I0553005

The Witch's Brew
Book 2

Brenda Cothern

By Brenda Cothern © 2019
All Rights Reserved.

ISBN-13: 978-1-943949-36-6
ISBN-10: 1-943949-36-0

First Printing April 2019

No part of this work may be copied, reproduced, altered, stored in a retrieval system or transmitted in any form, in any way, without prior, written permission from the author, except by a reviewer who may quote brief passages within the review for publication in a newspaper, magazine, journal, or on a website.

This story is a work of fiction. Names, characters, (some) places, and situations are the products of the author's imagination and intended to be fictional. Any resemblances to actual events, situations, or persons, alive or dead, are entirely coincidental.

This book contains M/M sexual situations is intended for readers of legal age in the country in which they reside. Please store your adult literature responsibly.

Wench Publishing, Inc.
136 E. 145th Avenue
Tampa, Florida, 33613

Other Titles

Shadows
Soul Stealer (FREE)
When Beasts Bite
Barely Restrained
Embracing Sin
Shattered Illusions

Guns & Hoses
Fire & Ice
Spark & Blaze
Then & Forever

I.N.E.T. 1
I.N.E.T. 2
I.N.E.T. 3
I.N.E.T. 4

The Witch's Brew 1
The Witch's Brew 2

Mad Dogs
Sixth
Deployed
Mad Dogs vol.1
Extraction
R&R
Mad Dogs vol.2
SNAFU
A.W.O.L.
Mad Dogs vol.3
Allies

Goddess of Fate
Retrieval
Reunion
Revelations

Those Who Dare
The Gardeners
Training for Revenge

Brothers by Bond
Undercover Love
Cresting Tide
New Beginnings
Coming Home
Before There Was Beer Pong

Dedication

To those who loved Shadows, The Witch's Brew
is for you.

Acknowledgments

My beta team, both those who have been with me
for several books and all of the new members who have
joined me for this one, you guys are incredible!
I love you guys!
Lora, Shirley, Danielle, & Melissa.
Without you, my writing wouldn't be nearly as
clean and the story would suffer.

Chapter One

The Witch's Brew was packed to capacity. It came as no surprise to any of the employees since it was Valentine's Day. Valentine's Day was their third busiest night after New Year's Eve and Halloween. All three holidays brought out more supernaturals than normals, but Mikael didn't mind. They spent money just like the norms and tended to be more behaved since they all understood the consequences if the norms discovered their community.

Mikael watched the crowd below from behind the glass that made up an entire wall of his office. His bartenders were running their asses off serving the three-deep crowd at each of his three bars. His waitresses were just as busy weaving through the crowd and dodging groping hands. The club security, in their neon yellow T-shirts, was easier to spot and Mikael's gaze only lingered for a moment longer on his lover, Adam, than it did the rest of his team who protected his patrons.

"Your first guest is here," George, his bear garoul doorman, informed him through his earpiece.

"Thank you, George. Please send them up."

Mikael had been looking forward to seeing his brothers and was actually surprised they were all able to accept his invitation on such a busy holiday. He was looking forward to catching up with Alec and Sebastian. A double tap knock sounded on his office door and

Mikael couldn't help the smile that spread his lips. Only his lover knocked on his office door in such a way.

"Enter," Mikael called out at the same time George informed him his other brother had arrived.

The door opened and Adam walked in followed closely by Alec and a beautiful woman who could only be Alec's wife, Kira. Alec confirmed the long-haired brunette was his wife when introductions were made.

"I'll return with your other brother," Adam smiled at his lover before he disappeared out the door, closing it behind him before Mikael could introduce him.

Less than five minutes later, there was another double tap on his office door. Adam didn't wait for permission to enter before he ushered Sebastian in. However, he didn't disappear to return back to his security station before Mikael had the opportunity to introduce him to his brothers.

Mikael offered refreshments to his brothers and they sat down to catch up. He wouldn't be able to introduce them to his adopted family until the club closed at three, but that would give them plenty of time to catch up beforehand. So, Mikael, Sebastian, and Alec and his wife did just that.

Travis had been running his ass off for hours. He may be a life drinker, Hollywood's version of a vampire even if 99% of what movies and TV portrayed was incorrect, but he was still tired. Not to mention his damn feet hurt. Of course, once the club closed and he had his meal, he would be fine.

Thinking of the nutrition he needed caused him to scan the club for that potential meal. The club would be closing soon, so if he was going to start flirting in order to get his dinner, now was the time to do so regardless of how he was still running up and down the bar serving drinks. Travis could just sate his hunger with Mikael's supply of blood or his own at home, but a fresh meal was sure to be available in the partying crowd.

Many others from their supernatural community had come out for Valentine's Day along with a plethora of norms. Any of them would feed him well, so he set to work charming those who might give him more than just a meal for the night.

Calvin gambled by coming to the Witch's Brew tonight. He had heard rumors that there was a community of his kind in Chicago and was more than relieved to find those rumors to be true when he sensed the garoul at the door to the club. Cal had no idea what type of garoul the large man shifted into, but he could sense he was large and possibly a predator.

It made Cal's inner cat hiss and desire to flee. As the smallest type of feline garoul, Cal's inner cat was more than skittish around larger garouls whether they were a predator or not. In fact, only birds and small mammals didn't set off his desire to run away and hide. No, they actually set off his own instinct to hunt. Tonight however, he pushed his feline side down so he could confirm there was a supernatural community in Chicago that wasn't just the Hunters he'd been hiding from for the last eight years.

His apprehension was high while he stood in line to enter the club, but once he passed the large garoul at the door and felt the presence of so many other supernaturals in the club, he relaxed. The garouls he could sense right away when he was close to them. They were all predators and he was sure they could sense him as well. They would sense that he could be prey. Still, that didn't dissuade him from heading directly to the bar on the left side of the club.

Cal also sensed a multitude of other supernaturals as he maneuvered through the crowd. He couldn't determine more, other than they weren't norms, but whatever they were, their presence only comforted him more. There was no way so many of the supernatural community here were all Hunters. Then again, some of them could be since there were always those who hated what they were and believed the cultish bullshit the Hunters spewed.

That thought not only made his feline hiss again, but also made his paranoia spike. Cal forced himself to push both down. He was here to enjoy himself which was something he'd yet to do since coming to Chicago almost a year ago.

If I just stick to my own community tonight, I should be fine, Cal reminded himself, since there tended to be more human Hunters than supernaturals who turned to their cause.

Cal finally made it to the bar. He stood between two norms that were leaning over the bar in an attempt to get the bartender's attention. The norms were both dressed the same even though one was a female and the other a male. Pink fairy like wings covered in glitter were strapped to their backs and the rest of their outfits were equally Valentine related colors. The woman wore a pink and white tutu and the man sported bright red pants. Both wore pale pink tank tops covered in solid red hearts.

Cal wasn't sure if the couple assumed their outfits were just what a Cupid would look like or not. In fact, they would have been cute if not for the silver, pink, and red glitter that rained off their wings every time they moved or were jostled by the crowd awaiting their turn to put in a drink order. Cal ignored the floating glints of glitter while the couple stood in front of him and instead tried to see the bartender. All he could see over the heads of the others at the bar was the dark head of a man who was in constant movement behind the bar.

Finally, the dark head of the bartender appeared in front of the two people to Cal's right. He still couldn't see more than the top of the man's head, but their proximity, even with the norms that stood between them, was enough to let Cal sense the bartender wasn't a norm.

A few minutes later, the plastic winged fairies in front of Cal moved. They shimmied away from the bar facing each other which gave Cal a full-frontal rub of the woman's wings. His black muscle shirt was now effectively covered with three different colors of glitter. Cal looked down and frowned as he stepped up to the bar into the now vacant space. The bartender had already moved down the line to the next waiting customers, but at least Cal now had a clear view of the man.

He had already sensed the man wasn't a norm just as he was able to sense other garouls, even if he couldn't identify their species. Cal pondered what the man actually was. However, it wasn't just Cal's curiosity over what type of supernatural would soon be serving him a drink which made him track the man as he fixed and delivered drinks. No, it was how breathtakingly attractive the man was that held Cal's attention. Dark hair, black if Cal had to guess even with the random club lights bouncing off the bartender, was cut short on the sides and back. Just enough of his hair was longer in the front to allow sweat to plaster it to the sides.

Likely from brushing it back from his face with his forearm, Cal thought.

Cal couldn't see the bartender's eyes, but he had no problem appreciating the man's body. Even from a distance, he could tell the bartender was a few inches taller than his five foot eleven. Muscles rippled on his bare arms and back every time the man poured a drink or set one down on the bar top. The guy was sleek, not bulky, even if he was larger in frame than Cal. Cal wasn't small either, not like a twink, so their builds were similar. The bartender was just Cal's type.

Then again, just because I am gay doesn't mean he is. Even, if this place is known to cater to the gay community, Cal reminded himself as he waited for the hot as hell bartender to reach him and take his drink order.

Travis glanced at the clock. 2:35. Ten minutes to last call and he was still running his ass off. So much so, he hadn't even had a pause long enough to flirt more than a smile or random wink. The chance of him having a fresh meal after his shift was slim to none at this rate. Of course, he knew it was wishful thinking to begin with since their busy holidays always turned out this way.

He sat down three drinks and had just picked up the cash for them before he turned to take the next order. That was when he caught sight of the blonde who stood next to his intended customer. The blonde's gaze met his before Travis shifted his attention to the burly man across the bar from him so he could take the drink order. Travis fully expected the man to order two drinks since the blonde was standing so close to the man. He was mildly surprised that wasn't the case when the man only ordered a rum and coke.

A single drink wasn't worth the trek down the bar to make, so he met the blonde's gaze again. "And what can I get for you, beautiful?"

Travis gave what he was sure was a garoul a smile and a wink. Maybe his chance for a fresh meal wasn't so far out of reach after all.

"Just a bottle of water," the blonde replied and Travis gave a nod before moving down the bar to fill the two orders.

Customers ordering water didn't faze Travis, so he didn't give it any thought when that was what the beautiful blonde ordered. What he did give thought to was if he'd ever seen the garoul in the Brew before tonight. He was pretty sure he hadn't because there was no way he would have forgotten a man who was that pretty.

Travis dropped off the rum and coke and took the burly man's cash. He was told to keep the change, but he hardly paid any attention to the man. His focus was on the blonde who picked up the bottle of water Travis had set down at the same time as the rum and Coke. The guy held out a five and it was more than enough to cover the bottle of water. Travis ignored it.

"On me." Travis gave the guy another wink before he shifted his body to take the order of the customer next to the attractive blonde.

Cal would've had to been blind not to recognize the bartender flirting with him. However, he couldn't continue to take up space at the bar because there were people very impatient for a drink behind him. So reluctantly, he stepped away from the bar.

Finding an empty space to stand wasn't easy, either, but once Cal spotted a section of empty wall he shuffled through the crowd to reach it. It was with a sigh of relief he leaned back against the black wall. He couldn't have planned his accidental space better since it gave him a perfect view of the bar lengthwise. Of course, all he could see of the hot bartender occasionally was his dark-haired head. That was just as well since even though he would like to take the supernatural up on his flirting, there was no way it would happen.

Maybe for just a one-night stand, the inner voice in Cal's mind tried to persuade him.

No, he couldn't risk it. It was bad enough he had to change crappy motels every few days to dodge the Hunters. He sure as hell wasn't going to put another supernatural in their sights. In his father's sights. Cal was sure the Hunters were well aware the Witch's Brew was frequented by supernaturals. However, he was equally sure they wouldn't try anything in the club. There were just too many supernaturals who partied here for the Hunters to attempt anything. It was Cal's faith in that assumption that gave him the courage to come to the club tonight. That and knowing it would likely be packed for Valentine's Day. The more people, supernaturals or norms, he could surround himself with the better chance he had of survival.

The club lights came on just as Cal took the last sip of his water. He hadn't looked away from the bar the entire time he stood plastered to the wall. The crowd had steadily thinned, but once the lights came on, they seemed to reluctantly shuffle away. It was obvious no more drinks would be served and it had everything to do with the DJ politely telling people the party was over.

The bartender was still hustling behind the bar, but Cal almost had an unobstructed view of the man now. Every time he caught sight of the supernatural through the slowly thinning crowd, Cal couldn't help but appreciate how attractive the man was. The temptation to linger and speak to him again was strong when their eyes met and another smile and wink was sent his way. God, that temptation was strong. Stronger still though was his resolve not to put a target from the Hunters on another supernatural's back. So, Cal returned the smile and reluctantly moved away from the wall the moment the bartender turned away. He had to force himself not to look back as he joined the horde leaving the club.

Travis had remained busy, but that didn't stop him from trying to spot the pretty blonde in the crowd. He had hoped the man would return to the bar to get another water, but that never happened. It wasn't until he was down to his diehard partiers who were determined to get one more drink at last call that he spotted the blonde leaning against the wall across from the short end of his bar. Travis almost missed seeing him since the man wore a black muscle shirt and equally black jeans. If it weren't for the guy's blonde hair, Travis might have missed him altogether.

He only had a few more customers to cash out, the Brew's regulars which Mikael trusted to run a tab, when the club lights came on. It was the first good look he had of the guy. It only confirmed what he'd seen under the dim club shadows, broken only by the dance floor lights, was an extremely beautiful man.

Travis gave the blonde another charmingly flirty smile and wink when their gazes met. He hoped it would be enough to entice the man to stick around until Travis could put off his closing duties and talk to him. Apparently, it wasn't because the next time Travis had the opportunity to look toward the wall, the man was gone. He did a quick scan of the crowd filing out the front door, but didn't spot a blonde head that might belong to the pretty man. Even if he had spotted the good-looking guy he hoped to do more with than just feed, it wasn't like he could go after him or have security stop him.

So much for a meal and maybe a good time, Travis thought when he turned back to cleaning up the mess of his customers' empty cups spewed all over his bar.

It was almost 5 AM when Mikael brought his guests down into the club. His human employees were already dismissed for the night. The garouls who he employed looked exhausted, so he only kept them long enough to introduce his family. Mikael sent Chris and Robert home as well. Adam and Randy retrieved barstools from the back and set them around the high tables Travis had pushed together. The life drinkers all took a seat and Travis offered to make them drinks.

"I'll take care of it," Mikael told his longtime friend and bartender. "You look beat."

Travis chuckled and tried not to look at his boss' brother, Sebastian. He had met Sebastian a few times since he and Mikael had become best friends. Each time, Travis was struck by how sexy the life drinker was and questioned if the man was flirting with him or not. Sebastian's behavior toward him wasn't overt, so even as old as they both were, Travis couldn't tell. Since the man was Mikael's brother, Travis wasn't going to assume anything one way or the other. He'd leave the ball in Sebastian's court if the man wanted to mess around. Still, Travis would definitely catch that ball if it was tossed his way.

Travis shook his thoughts of Mikael's brother from his mind. "I am tired, but nothing a good meal won't fix."

"I would've thought with your looks, you would have your choice from the crowd tonight," Sebastian commented in a neutral tone.

Once again, Travis couldn't tell if the life drinker was flirting or not. It was frustrating to say the least and he was tempted to reply with a flirty comeback, but he didn't.

"It was too busy to secure something solid." Travis finally looked at Sebastian. "I can only flirt so much while I am running my ass off." Sebastian smiled and Travis wished he knew if the man was just being polite or if there was more to his comment.

"Here we go," Mikael said and started placing drinks down in front of everyone from the tray he held.

The life drinkers and Alec's wife got to know one another over the next three hours. They didn't sleep, so there was no need to rush off to bed in order to get some rest. Still, not needing to sleep didn't mean they couldn't become tired. And Travis was just that.

"As nice as this is, I'm going to call it a night," Travis said even though 8 AM was considered morning to most of the world. "I need to eat, but I am sure I'll see all of you again before you leave town." Travis gave them all a smile and stood.

"Let us give you a ride," Alec offered and stood with his wife.

"That's not necessary, but I'll accept." Travis smiled at Mikael's brother and once more tried to ignore Sebastian's large form standing as well.

12

"We will see you tomorrow, then," Mikael said by way of goodbye.

"Would you like a ride as well, Randy?" Alec asked Mikael's bar manager.

"Thank you, but no. I am fine," Randy declined politely.

The group finished saying their goodbyes and Travis followed Alec, Kira, and Sebastian's sexy ass out the back door of the club to their SUV.

Chapter Two

Travis climbed into the back seat of the SUV and sat next to Sebastian. The heat radiating off the man was almost palpable. Hollywood portrayed life drinkers, vampires as they called their kind, as cold, undead creatures which was so far from the truth it was almost funny. Their kind wouldn't survive long amongst the norms if any time a norm rubbed against them it felt like they were brushing an ice cube. Still, the heat Travis felt coming off Sebastian *was* hot. It only made Travis' tiredness feel all the more pronounced and his desire to feed in order to alleviate the sensation stronger.

"Where are we taking you, Travis?" Alec glanced in the rearview mirror to look at him.

"Thirty-fourth and..."

"You could dine with me, if you'd like," Sebastian interrupted before Travis could finish giving Alec his address.

Travis looked at Sebastian and was greeted with the same smile he hadn't been able to interpret whenever they've met over the last three hundred years. However, Sebastian inviting him to enjoy a meal was a clear sign the man was lobbing the ball into his side of the court.

"I'd like that." Travis gave Sebastian a charming smile. "Very much."

"Good," Sebastian replied evenly.

"To the hotel then," Alec commented, but Travis had no problem seeing the older life drinker's smile in the rearview mirror.

Travis said good night to Alec and his wife before he followed Sebastian into his suite. He wasn't sure what to expect from Sebastian, but he was sure this offer of a shared meal was more than just that.

"I'll order room service," Sebastian informed as he removed his suit jacket and draped it over a chair in the salon area. "Do you have a preference for what you'd like to have?"

"Whatever food you wish to order is fine since that isn't the meal I desire." Travis smiled and took a seat on the sofa.

Sebastian chuckled and picked up the phone to order room service. Once he was done, he removed his cufflinks and rolled up his shirt cuffs. He was getting comfortable and Travis liked seeing this side of the man. He liked it even more when Sebastian took a seat next to him on the couch.

Sebastian folded one of his slack covered legs under the other when he sat facing Travis. His arm rested along the back of the sofa, stretched out far enough that he could easily caress the nape of Travis' neck if he chose to do so.

"I can't seem to figure you out, Travis," Sebastian said almost with a tone of curiosity.

"What do you mean?" Travis was genuinely intrigued by Sebastian's comment.

Travis was outgoing and friendly. Loyal to a fault where his friends and chosen family were concerned. So, he really wasn't sure what Sebastian had a problem with in figuring him out.

"I've seen you flirt freely with norms and those of our community. I have also read your interest in me, but yet you have refrained from showering me with those same advances." Sebastian smiled. "There is a welcoming desire in your gaze when you look at me," Sebastian continued knowingly. "So, I can't help but wonder if you hold back because I intimidate you or because I am Mikael's brother."

Travis just stared at the man. How could Sebastian not realize he didn't send out any indications he was interested in more than polite socialization?

"I am not intimidated by you and we both know Mikael wouldn't care if we enjoyed each other's company," Travis stated what he felt was obvious. At least to him.

"Is it our age difference, then? Because after so many centuries, age is little more than a number regardless of how our longevity increases our powers."

Sebastian seemed totally sincere in his inquiry. Still, that didn't stop Travis from laughing at the absurdity the man thought he was bothered by the few centuries that separated them.

"No, the difference in our age doesn't bother me at all because I agree with you." Travis returned Sebastian smile.

"What then?" Sebastian raised an inquiring brow.

"You are impossible to read and as we've only seen each other a few dozen times since I met Mikael, I had no idea you were interested in a little fun."

"Really?" Sebastian inquired sincerely and Travis just chuckled.

There was a soft knock on the suite door before Travis could make a reply. That was just fine by him because he really didn't wish to continue their current conversation. There wasn't a need to now that he was aware Sebastian wanted to have some fun. Right now, Travis wanted to feed, but that didn't mean he wasn't appreciating the view of Sebastian's slack covered ass while the man crossed the suite to answer the door.

Sebastian opened the door and was pleased to see a young man standing behind a food cart. The hotel employee was attractive. Attractive indeed, but even if he wasn't he would still provide the meal Travis needed.

"Your meal, sir," the young man announced as if the food cart didn't make his order obvious.

"Please, come in." Sebastian stepped back to allow the hotel employee entrance into his suite.

The young man whose name plate said 'Greg' didn't hesitate to push the cart into the room. As the cart passed Sebastian, he could easily smell the steak Tartar and rare burgers even though they were covered with silver food domes. After the food cart was placed precisely next to the suite's dining room table, Greg turned to face Sebastian. Greg met Sebastian's gaze as he waited for his expectant tip. Sebastian smiled at the young man politely.

"You would like to stay for a while," Sebastian said softly.

Greg's eyes slightly glazed over before he replied, "I'd like to stay a while."

Sebastian continued to smile. His kind, especially one of his age, could easily manipulate a norm's mind unless they were extremely mentally strong. Most norms were not. However, if the young hotel employee had replied along the lines of having to return to work, Sebastian would have let him. It was easy enough to find take-out for Travis had that been the case. It wasn't, though.

Sebastian caught sight of Travis standing from the couch, but didn't track his fellow life drinker's movement. He didn't even meet Travis' gaze until the man stood behind Greg.

Travis pressed his chest against the young man's back and breathed in deeply. It didn't escape his notice when the hotel employee entered Sebastian's suite that the man was attractive. He was attractive enough that had Sebastian not been interested in some fun, Travis would sate a totally different hunger with the norm.

He hadn't had sex in a while even though the bite of their kind caused immense pleasure for those they fed upon. He just hadn't been interested enough with his last few fresh meals to bother. Still, that didn't mean the young man wouldn't enjoy this experience even though Travis wouldn't push extra pleasure into his bite.

"He smells delicious," Travis whispered over the norm's shoulder. He knew Sebastian understood he was referring to the clean scent of the man's blood and not the cologne the guy wore.

"Bon Appétit." Sebastian smiled.

Travis ran his hands in a soft caress over the white uniform jacket the norm wore. The man shivered under his touch even though there was stiff cloth preventing skin on skin contact. He stopped when he met Greg's wrist and lifted one arm toward Sebastian while he stepped to the side behind the young man's back.

Sebastian accepted the wrist Travis offered, but didn't wish to feed. He was more interested in watching Travis as his fellow life drinker pushed up the cuff of Greg's uniform to bare the man's wrist. Gently, Travis brought his other hand up to cup the young man's wrist. Only the briefest glimpse of fangs were revealed, before Travis leaned forward at the same time he raised the norms wrist to his mouth and he struck.

Travis didn't break eye contact with Sebastian while he fed. The clean syrupy taste of the norm's blood coated his throat and spread additional warmth through him. Feeding was always erotic when he took a meal from a norm. It always turned him on whether he planned to have sex with his meal or not.

However, seeing the first flash of desire in Sebastian's pale blue gaze as the older life drinker watched him feed was more arousing than anything Travis had felt recently. The look of hunger in Sebastian's eyes only reinforced Travis' decision that he wasn't going to take much from the hotel employee. He had already planned to only feed enough to mute the edge of his hunger. Travis could have a full meal from his supply at home and right now he didn't want to ignore the pressure in his jeans any longer.

Sebastian couldn't mistake the look of hunger in Travis' gray eyes. It was an intense gaze that didn't have a damn thing to do with the nourishment he was currently consuming. His smile slowly spread wider while he watched Travis pull back and lick the norms wrist to close the wound he'd inflicted.

"It took a few minutes for us to open the door, then you used the restroom before you returned to work," Sebastian informed Greg and waited for him to nod. Once the man did, Sebastian escorted him to the door.

Sebastian turned toward Travis who hadn't moved. He took the few steps toward the younger life drinker until he stopped before the man.

"What do you want, now?" Sebastian inquired. "Food or..."

"Or," Travis replied and barely had time to brace himself before Sebastian pulled him close and plundered his mouth.

Travis didn't resist in the slightest. No, his hands responded just as aggressively as his mouth met Sebastian's onslaught. Buttons popped and flew when Travis grasped and pulled Sebastian's dress shirt open in order to feel skin. Travis moaned when he felt bare skin beneath his palms.

Sebastian felt his dress shirt destroyed, but didn't give a shit. He was too focused on the taste of Travis and getting the man's jeans open so he could feel the hardness in his hand that he felt through Travis' denim.

Finally, Travis thought when he felt Sebastian take him in hand. Unbeknownst to him, Sebastian had the same thought.

Sebastian groaned into their kiss when he felt the weight of Travis' member in his hand. Travis' size only turned him on more. Sebastian had no shame when it came to admitting he liked large cocks. Travis *was* large, too. His fingers didn't touch around Travis's girth, so the life drinker was at least four inches around. The fact that he could encase Travis in the palm of his hand and couldn't feel the man's bulbous head against him only confirmed Travis was more than seven inches long. Just the thought of having Travis buried deep inside him made him groan again.

Travis had been walking them backwards toward the couch. Sebastian's hand wrapping firmly around his cock practically made him desperate to cum. He pushed the feeling down deep because he wasn't about to blow his load until he was buried deep in Sebastian or Sebastian in him. Still, that didn't stop Travis from frantically unbuttoning Sebastian's belt, pushing the man's slacks lower on his hips, and grasping his fellow life drinker's cock.

Sebastian hissed at the first touch of Travis' calloused hand when it wrapped around his length. He had no choice other than to pull out of their all absorbing kiss.

"Bedroom," Sebastian panted out against Travis' lips at the same time he thrust his hips forward to cause his dick to slide in Travis' hand.

"Too far," Travis replied because he didn't think he'd last that long and felt the side of the couch against the side of his knee.

So, instead of saying anything more or allowing Sebastian the opportunity to answer, Travis spun the older life drinker toward the couch. Gravity did what gravity does and Travis winced when Sebastian's hand pulled on his cock before he let go and fell onto the couch.

Sebastian fought to catch his breath. He'd been doing so since the moment his lips touched Travis' luscious mouth. Now, he looked up at the younger life drinker and couldn't help his gaze from zeroing in on the beautifully large cock jutting out from the black jeans Travis wore. Sebastian was so focused on what he desired to feel inside of him that he gave no notice to the fact that Travis was fully dressed otherwise. He finally looked up from where he landed on the couch and met Travis' desire blown pupils.

"What do you want?" Sebastian asked again with no shame. Whatever position, top or bottom, Travis wanted didn't matter. Life drinker's as old as they both were had done it all and more than likely enjoyed either.

"In you," Travis stated plainly in a lust graveled voice. "To feel you wrapped around me."

Sebastian was moving before Travis had even finished speaking. He lifted his hips and shimmied his slacks down some more before he turned around to bend over the back of the couch. His slacks would prevent him from spreading his legs too wide, but that would only make his ass all the tighter for Travis.

The second Sebastian pushed his slacks down further; Travis spit in his palm and stroked his cock to spread his improvised lube. Spit wasn't lube, but that didn't stop him from spitting again on Sebastian's hole once the older life drinker was in position. He wouldn't use spit as lube on a norm. They didn't have the healing ability their kind possessed and it was because of this Travis didn't hesitate to push into Sebastian's tight heat. A deep moan of satisfaction surrounded them and Travis wasn't sure if it came from him or Sebastian. Not that it mattered as he sunk hilt deep.

The total fullness was heaven for Sebastian. The stretch and burn from using only spit as lube was more than welcome. He wasn't sure if he felt another drop of spit on his hole before he felt Travis pull back. It didn't matter, though. In fact, feeling Travis spit on him wasn't even a solid thought when the younger life drinker began to move.

Sebastian was tight. So, fucking tight. The additional spit Travis spat down on where his cock was buried hilt deep didn't make a damn bit of difference for the ease of his movement when he pulled back and thrust forward again harshly. He could feel the skin along his cock stretch and contract with every thrust, but that feeling, that slight twinge of pain, didn't stop him from pounding into Sebastian's incredibly tight channel.

Sebastian pushed back into every thrust Travis pounded against his ass. The slightest arch of his back while he grasped the back of the couch had Travis nailing his prostate. Repeatedly. It took less than a dozen thrusts from Travis before he stiffened and his orgasm barreled explosively out of the head of his cock.

Travis felt the moment Sebastian crashed over the edge of orgasm. He didn't even need to touch the older life drinker's cock before he felt Sebastian's ass clamp down around him. Still, Travis pushed through the clamp that was now Sebastian's ass. The resistance was just enough that after a few thrusts, Travis joined Sebastian in orgasmic bliss.

He crashed down onto Sebastian's dress shirt covered back and panted to catch his breath. Travis gave no thought to the sweat soaking through Sebastian's shirt or his own tank top. No, Travis was just grateful Sebastian had the forethought to brace his chest over the back of the couch. Otherwise, the older life drinker would have had no choice but to be bent in an extremely uncomfortable position.

Travis' breath finally settled while his forehead pressed against the nape of Sebastian's neck which was covered with the man's sweaty long black hair. Slowly, Travis stood upright and pulled out of Sebastian. His action was greeted with a groan. However, that didn't stop him from stepping back a few feet and tucking himself away.

Sebastian didn't want to move even after he felt Travis vacate his body. So, he remained in place, Travis stepped away even though he had no reason to do so. Sebastian wasn't worried about any uncomfortableness that would normally follow a hook up. No, he was just comfortably mellow and didn't want to move yet. He heard Travis' zipper, so he knew the younger life drinker had righted himself after their bit of fun.

"That was good," Sebastian commented. "I needed that." He finally forced himself to turn and flop his semi sore ass down on the couch.

Travis couldn't stop the smile that spread his lips at seeing Mikael's brother so nonchalantly settle on the couch. The man didn't seem to give any thought to his limp dick that now rested to the side of his open slacks.

"I did, too," Travis replied and waited for Sebastian to say more.

He wasn't expecting an invitation to spend the rest of the day in the suite with Sebastian. In fact, he was grateful when the older life drinker didn't reply or offer an invitation to do so.

"How long will you be in town?" Travis asked in a tone which was more curious than one that indicated he was interested in a repeat.

"I'll likely be leaving tonight," Sebastian replied. "I can't leave the Brew in California unattended for too long."

"That's understandable." Travis could sympathize since he was aware of how attentive Mikael was to their club in Chicago. "I'm heading home," Travis stated without feeling as if he was blowing Sebastian off. "I'll see you next time you're in town."

Travis walked toward the door and opened it before he glanced back to the still half naked older life drinker. "Tonight, was fun. Don't be so unreadable for the next few centuries and we can do this again sometime."

Sebastian grinned. "That we can." He gave Travis a nod and was still smiling when his brother's employee disappeared out of his suite door.

The thought of the food on the cart had never crossed either man's mind.

Chapter Three

Cal closed the door behind him and tried to ignore the interior of his shitty motel room. It wasn't as if he weren't used to living in dives that catered more to drug dealers and street workers. Still, every time he came back to whatever shithole he was staying at from whatever temporary shit job he held, he just couldn't help but feel like his life could get any worse. Of course, it could. He could end up dead and that would definitely be worse.

He had no doubt if the current group of hunters in Chicago led by his human father, he was sure, found him he would end up dead. His father had killed his mother, after all, and hunted him down ever since. She'd still be alive if it weren't for his sperm donor.

Guilt weighed him down over shifting for the first time when he hit puberty even though his rational mind tried to convince him that his mother's murder wasn't his fault. If he hadn't shifted, if his father hadn't seen him, the bastard would never have known he or she were shifters.

It didn't matter to Cal that his mother kept her true self from him and his father. He understood she was happy and in love with the man. However, her keeping him ignorant until Cal shifted at puberty only proved his father didn't love her, and by extension him, to the same degree.

Zombielike, Cal walked further into the crappy motel room he currently called home. He couldn't stay at this dump much longer, but that thought didn't really register when he was assaulted by memories from ten years ago.

His illness was horrible. His body ached and his skin felt too tight as if something was boiling beneath the surface and pressing to escape. Mom took care of him. Told him everything would be okay and he would be fine. He didn't believe her even though she convinced dad it was a bad case of the flu. Dad was worried and insisted he see a doctor, but mom never took him. She lied to dad. Said she did, but he was too ill to say otherwise.

Repeatedly, mom told him he'd be okay. She told him a lot of things which made him think she was crazy. And he did think she was crazy. Crazy and totally insane. Until that was the pressure inside of him seemed to explode.

One moment, mom was dabbing his forehead with a damp cloth then the next he felt no sickness at all. No, he felt cured. Felt alive. The pressure and tightness which seemed to stretch his skin to the point of pain was just gone. However, even if his pain was gone and he felt cured, his vision was fucked. Everything appeared in shades of blue and gray. In his panic, he yelled, but the sound that escaped his throat was a high-pitched meow.

His mother was attempting to calm and comfort him, to explain what was happening, but the noise he made drew the attention of his father.

Cal huddled against the headboard of his bed and witnessed his father storm into the room to investigate. Scared, not only because he wasn't sure what was happening to him, but also at his mother's attempt to explain to his father, he bolted toward the barely cracked window.

The body he found himself in was not his own. It was something else. He didn't know what until his mother tried to explain to his father. He learned a lot from her explanation and his fear began to subside. Until, his father became violent.

Back arched and hair standing on end, he listened to his father accuse his mother of being an abomination and by extension he being one as well. She argued. She tried to explain. Still, that didn't stop the violence that raged through his father.

The beating, fists pummeling against her small frame, until she shifted kept him frozen to the spot where he perched on the sill of the open window in his bedroom. His father was still panting from the exertion of trying to kill his mother before she shifted when his father turned toward him.

"You both need to die. I won't have the devils who tricked me still breathe."

His father ignored his mother and lunged at him. Instinctively, he squeezed his body through the cracked window and bolted away.

"I'll find you, boy! No spawn of mine from the devil will live!"

The shout and declaration from his father echoed in his ears while he ran away from the only home he'd ever known. It was two days before his mother found him.

Cal shook himself free of the memories from his past. It was something he was intimately used to doing even though the memories were more than a decade old. He always counted those memories from when he heard his mother's explanation to his father about what he was and their flight with the memories of how fortunate they were to survive those first several years unmolested.

Originally, he thought his father had finally forgotten about him and his mother. He was relieved at that thought even if it proved to be wrong. After eight years his father finally tracked them down and he witnessed the man kill his mother. He lived on the streets after that and struggled to survive. He did so by remaining in his cat form. It wasn't until he was twenty and befriended a blind man while in his cat form that he was finally able to make something of himself in the human world.

Abe took him in as a stray cat, but seemed to instinctively know he was something more. The old man would talk to him as if he were human during the day and Cal decision to risk revealing his human self, was life-changing. Abe was beyond pleased to find out the stray cat he'd adopted was more than just an abandoned animal. In fact, Abe seemed to love him even more.

He encouraged Cal to be true to himself and live life to the fullest. Abe paid for his college and when the kind old man died after two years of treating him like a son, Abe left him everything. Abe's estate was enough to allow Cal to live comfortably, but within a month of his adopted father's death, several seemingly innocent accidents seem to befall him. It took five near misses that could've killed him before he realized they weren't accidents at all.

Some subtle investigation revealed the hunters who wanted to eradicate anyone not human. It wasn't a large leap of logic to determine his father had found such a group. So even though he had money to live comfortably, he felt safer living in dives which he now called home. However, he couldn't help but smile as he stepped into the shower and thought about finally daring to follow the rumors that led him to the Witch's Brew. Those rumors said his kind would be welcoming. Thinking of the sexy as hell bartender didn't hurt at all, either.

The first thing Travis did when he arrived home was to have a meal from his blood supply. Once he finished a bag of warmed O positive, Travis attended to his other hunger. He thought of the delicious smelling hotel food he and Sebastian never got around to eating while his Italian stew warmed up on the stove. His stew was likely just as gourmet as the hotel food. A few centuries of life had taught him how to be an excellent cook.

However, once he began to eat, his thoughts turned away from food and back to Sebastian. Travis had known Mikael's brother for centuries, so he couldn't help but wonder why the man finally wanted to mess around. Not that Travis was complaining because he sure as hell wasn't.

For some reason the thought of having some fun with Sebastian made Travis think of the pretty blonde he'd seen close to closing time the previous night. The blonde was by far more his type regardless of how sexy he found Sebastian. His mind was still on the beautiful blonde after he washed his bowl and walked into his library. Well, the second largest bedroom in his house that he'd turned into a library.

A few thousand books filled the space. Most were on the floor-to-ceiling bookshelves he'd built when he'd moved in, but there were several stacks littered around as well. The only other items in the room were two antique lamps on just as antique tables bracketing his modern and extremely comfortable couch.

Travis spent most of his time in this room. Almost every book in the room was a first edition. Some of them were even signed by the authors. Those were worth more, but Travis gave no thought to their monetary value even though his collection was worth several billions. He had billions of dollars in each of his several bank accounts spread around the world, so the millions he could acquire by selling his collection never even crossed his mind.

Plus, he loved to read. His entire life he'd loved to read. Any subject was just fine by him. Of course, even though he owned much older books, those from the Renaissance were by far his favorite. There was just something he loved about the way the authors from the fourteenth through the seventeenth centuries told their stories. His love for those books most likely had everything to do with them being from his childhood than anything else, but he rarely gave that any thought.

However, as he pulled Sir Thomas More's Utopia off his shelf, it really wasn't his childhood that crossed his mind. Well, not so much as his childhood as he lay on his couch, but his age. He was still young for a life drinker, but had no doubt he was older than any garoul he currently knew. They only lived a few hundred years and weren't immortal like his kind. Garouls did age if a bit slowly. It was that thought that brought him back to the pretty blonde garoul he'd served last night. The guy looked young compared to his garoul co-workers. His thoughts instantly sparked his curiosity over the man's age.

Travis hoped the garoul would come back to the Brew sometime and he would actually get the opportunity to speak to the beautiful blonde, but only time would tell if that happened. So, he pushed his thoughts of the guy from his mind as he began to read one of his books which he already knew word for word.

Cal was dressed casually in jeans and a T-shirt when he was dropped off in front of the building nearest to the Witch's Brew. It was just after 3 AM so he knew the club was already closed when he stepped into the shadows to shift.

For the last two weeks he couldn't stop thinking about the dark-haired bartender. He wanted to see the supernatural again even though he refused to put a hunter target on the attractive man's back. That was precisely why he hadn't returned to the club to fulfill his desire for another look. However, three days ago he realized he had the perfect solution to getting another view of the man. Well, almost a perfect solution. All clubs had trash and his years on the streets taught him the dumpsters were always located behind the businesses.

Cats, feral cats, were seen all the time scrounging around them for food. Granted, he'd never seen another calico cat prowling around them, but he was sure humans gave no thought to the different looking cats seeking out scraps. In fact, most of his experience around dumpsters and the humans who owned them was being chased away. Not that he didn't return once they were gone.

Cal had no idea if the bartender he wished to see would be the employee who brought out the club's trash. Cal would still have to remain hidden to get his glimpse even if the employee tasked with the chore wasn't the bartender he wished to see. If he could tell the guy wasn't a norm than he was sure the sexy bartender had sensed the same about him. The man worked in a bar supernaturals frequented, after all. Still, that wouldn't ensure he would sense Cal tonight and even if he did, Cal wouldn't shift back to reveal himself.

The three dumpsters behind the club came in sight when he rounded the corner. He bolted toward them and was relieved they were the type that had legs to keep them slightly off the ground. He chose the middle dumpster to crawl under. The space for these types of dumpsters was always tight. Still, he'd hidden beneath this kind before so he had no problem belly crawling underneath. The stench of sour alcohol was strong, but not the worst smell he'd ever encountered while hiding under a dumpster.

Cal settled into position and watched the back door of the club. He hoped he would see the attractive supernatural bartender he couldn't stop thinking about. In fact, he kept repeating in his mind; *let it be him taking out the trash.*

Travis always offered to take out the night's garbage. His fellow bartenders, Jules and Barb were respectively a fae and garoul, and even though they had extended lifespans Travis understood they would always feel the exhaustion of their shift more than he ever would. He loved both of the women he'd known for little more than a hundred years. Taking care of the trash was no big deal for him since he didn't need to sleep and they did.

"Night, Travis," Jules called out.

"See you tomorrow," Barb added while George walked them toward the front door of the Brew.

Their head of security always walked out the female employees before he left for the night. Barb and Jules were usually the last of them to go for the evening, so Travis knew the bear garoul wouldn't be returning to the club after he locked the front door behind them.

Mikael and Adam had already retired for the night. It was their normal routine and Travis gave no thought to being alone in the club when he started grabbing the trash. It wouldn't take him long to carry the several bags out back to the dumpsters, but he wasn't in a hurry. His dinner, pot roast and mashed potatoes and his books would still be there when he got home.

Travis picked up two bags which were full of empty beer bottles and other trash. He only set one down before he punched in the security code to the back door. After pushing the door open and holding it that way with his hip, he picked up the second bag of trash again. Less than a dozen steps brought him to the dumpster to the right of him. He lifted the lid and slung the bags over the lip of the dumpster. Those were the last two bags that would fit in that particular dumpster.

Travis had the habit of filling each dumpster equally. He frowned because he knew there was no way the lid on the third dumpster would close all the way after tonight's trash was taken out. Thankfully, the dumpster company would be coming to empty them tomorrow. They rarely had a problem with critters getting into their trash, but that didn't mean they sometimes didn't. Cleaning up the mess they made while they scavenged for food was a pain in the ass and one Travis didn't relish.

Those were his thoughts while he carried two more bags out the back door before tossing them into the middle dumpster. They landed with the shattering clang he was used to hearing, but another noise reached his sensitive ears. It was one he recognized even if he seldom heard it.

Cal still startled when the bags of beer bottles connected with the other trash in the dumpster. He had lived on the streets for years, but still reacted the same way. Cal had watched the dark-haired bartender throw away two bags in the dumpster to his left and even though he watched the man walk toward the dumpster he hid beneath to throw away the next two bags of bar trash, Cal still reacted as if this was his first time hiding under a dumpster.

His body jolted from the noise and connected with the underside of the dumpster. He froze at the same time as the hot bartender cocked his head to the side. Cal had no doubt the supernatural heard him when his body connected with the underside of the dumpster. He attempted to remain quiet by panting softly through his mouth. However, he couldn't remain in his current position because if the attractive bartender looked under the dumpster, he would be clearly seen. So, he crawled backwards as silently as his small padded paws would allow.

Cal could only see the bartender's feet now, but he was okay with that. Too many times he had had to escape violent norms while he tried to find a meal from a dumpster. His reaction was instinctive despite his knowing the bartender wasn't a norm. He couldn't stop the memories from flooding his mind of past experiences with norms discovering him and the violence he sometimes suffered as a result. Cal didn't think the bartender would become violent, but he didn't know the supernatural from Adam, so it was always a possibility.

Cal was still trying to pant quietly as he waited for the bartender to do something other than stand in front of the dumpster he was hiding beneath. His bob-tailed ass was practically clear of the back of the dumpster and Cal was sure he could continue backing out before fleeing. So, he stared at the supernatural's sneakered covered feet and prepared to bolt if he saw any movement that didn't indicate the sexy bartender was going to do anything other than turn around and go back into the club.

The additional sound Travis heard clearly indicated an animal was under the Brew's dumpster. He listened for the animal to make another noise while he stilled as not to scare it. His sensitive ears heard the slow movement of the animal moving toward the rear of the dumpster.

In the past when he'd encountered cats, raccoons, or possums, the animals fled the moment he startled them. This critter didn't do that, but rather attempted to make a stealthy retreat further back under the dumpster in order to stay hidden or to protect itself. Only something intelligent would do that, so Travis breathed in deep.

The smell of the bar trash was prominent, but didn't prevent Travis from detecting the slight scent all garouls emitted. He had no way to identify more than a garoul was currently hiding under the Brew's dumpster, but that didn't matter to Travis. The garoul was obviously afraid, but the garoul's fear wasn't about to stop Travis from helping him or her. So, he made the decision to return to the bar for two more bags of trash in hopes his walking away would lessen the garoul's fear of him.

Chapter Four

Cal breathed a mental sigh of relief the moment he witnessed the bartender's sneaker covered feet finally move and walk away. He didn't move away from where he was crouched under the backside of the dumpster, though.

He doubted the club only had four bags of trash that needed to be taken out. Cal was sure there were more, so he stayed put and watched intently for the bartender's sneakers to make another appearance. His ears were also pitched forward so he could hear the sound of the club's back door opening again.

Cal heard nor saw either which was precisely why he startled. His body jumped the few scant inches between him and the dumpster a few moments later.

Travis was determined to help what he was more than sure was a garoul scared and hiding under the Brew's middle dumpster. Thoughts of the remaining trash he had to take out were replaced by what he could do to help the garoul. He was sure the garoul wasn't aware he was not alone in the world if for no other reason than his behavior.

Travis couldn't think of any reason a garoul would be foraging for food around the dumpster. Garouls cared about family more passionately than any other supernaturals he had ever encountered before in his long lifetime. They weren't left to fend for themselves, so why this one was he had no idea.

However, it was more than apparent the lone garoul wasn't aware of their supernatural world based on their behavior when he approached the dumpster. Travis couldn't even comprehend how that was possible since all supernaturals had the ability to discern the difference between them and norms. Still, there could be the off chance this wasn't the case with this particular garoul even if it was extremely unlikely.

Perhaps, this garoul experienced some sort of trauma with someone from the supernatural community. It wouldn't be the first encounter Travis came across where this was the case. This was exactly why he left the club and approached the dumpster from the side instead of head on if he had exited through the back door. He wanted to ensure the garoul didn't feel penned in by him as he might if Travis stood in front of the dumpsters.

Travis moved silently. He normally didn't make an effort to do so. He could shadow step to reach the side of the dumpsters, since the back of the Brew provided him enough shadows. However, he wanted to approach normally so he wouldn't scare the garoul even more than he already had.

He stopped near the back of the first dumpster in the row that the Brew owned. Looking behind them showed him the barest glimpse of white. Travis remained quiet while his eyes adjusted to what looked like a soft covered fur. What he saw was definitely not a raccoon or possum garoul since he couldn't see a tail. A white bobtail was what Travis could see and the only animals he was aware of that were fur covered and had no tail were cats. Cats, the domestic looking kind, were almost the smallest garouls after birds and some rare smaller mammals.

It's no wonder they are frightened all to shit, Travis thought as he decided how to proceed.

Smaller garouls were always more skittish than their larger kind in Travis's experience. That came as no surprise since they could be prey for almost anyone in the supernatural community. The garoul hidden under the Brew's dumpster may already feel that was the case if he was aware of the supernatural community.

No one at the Brew, whether they work there or were a patron, would prey on the smaller garoul cat. Travis just needed a way to convince him or her of that. Being alone or feeling that way and scared was no way to live. Especially, since garouls could live for a few hundred years. Just the thought this garoul had been living that way for a while made Travis' chest tighten and his heart break. So much so, that he was determined to do something about it.

"You can come out," Travis said softly after he squatted down. "I won't hurt you. You are safe here."

The sound of the bartender's voice coming from near the dumpster to his left startled Cal badly. His body once again connected with the underside of the dumpster. Instinctively, he belly crawled away. Cal didn't stop moving until he was sure he was underneath the center of the dumpster. It was a location experience told him he'd be safe from being reached by grabby hands trying to pull him out.

Travis wasn't surprised to see the bobtail end of the cat garoul disappear under the dumpster. He understood addressing the garoul would likely cause him or her to bolt further under the dumpster they hid beneath even though there was a dumpster separating them from the garoul's hiding place. Still, that didn't stop him from talking to the cat garoul he'd accidentally come across while taking out the Brew's trash.

"I won't hurt you," Travis repeated and waited patiently to see any flash of white fur that would indicate the garoul would leave its hiding place.

Several minutes passed and Travis saw no sign of the white-tailed bobcat. He wasn't sure what else to do, aside from keep talking to the garoul. He hoped that would be enough to lure the garoul out but he doubted the sound of his gentle voice and sincere words would work. Still, that didn't stop Travis from trying.

"You're not alone," Travis started. "Let me help you. I promise you will be safe. Just come out. Please."

Cal couldn't mistake the bartender's tone for anything else but what it was: sincere concern for him. It flooded his entire being with warmth. He hadn't heard that level of concern since before his father killed his mother. Memories of the day his father had finally tracked them down threatened to overwhelm him, but he pushed them away.

The bartender was still trying to coax him out and Cal was tempted to leave the safety of his hiding spot. However, he didn't know the sexy supernatural. Cal couldn't stop his paranoia from rising that the man who had filled his mind since he dared to come to the Witch's Brew on Valentine's Day could be a Hunter. There was no way which he was aware of to tell the difference

42

between those who believed the cult shit of the Hunters and those who didn't.

It was that paranoia that had kept him alive since his father killed his mother. It kept him securely hidden in a spot underneath the dumpster where he couldn't be reached, as well.

"I know you're scared, but you have nothing to fear from me." Travis continued to coax the cat garoul out. After several more minutes of not seeing the cat, Travis continued, "you don't have a reason to trust me, but I understand." Travis paused once again. "So, come back tomorrow night. I'll bring you some food so you don't need to dumpster dive. The Witch's Brew is the safest place for you since there are other garouls who work here also."

Cal was already aware of the garouls and other supernaturals that frequented the Witch's Brew, but that knowledge didn't trump his sudden fear that the sexy dark-haired bartender could be a Hunter. For all Cal knew, the supernaturals and other garouls could be Hunters who just lured others into the club.

Why he hadn't thought of that when he followed the rumors to the Witch's Brew to find a community where he'd be safe, he didn't know. However, the thought now blindsided him and petrified him in place regardless of the hot bartender's words and tone of voice.

The fact that the garoul still hadn't made an appearance from under the dumpster in which he hid told Travis getting them to come out just wasn't going to happen. At least not tonight. All Travis could hope for was that he didn't scare the garoul enough that he wouldn't return again. He knew enough about garouls to know they couldn't remain in their shifted forms for more than twenty-four hours before they became feral.

The cat garoul's behavior proved he wasn't feral because if he or she were, the garoul would have bolted like any other wild animal once he started talking. Still, just because the garoul wasn't feral didn't mean they weren't homeless and more than likely starving if they were visiting dumpsters in search of food.

"I have a few more bags of trash to bring out, but you can stay where you are unless you want to leave while I am inside. Still, I'll bring you something to eat tomorrow night if you want to come back," Travis said sincerely before he stood and disappeared through the back door of the club.

Cal remained hunched down in his safe space under the center of the dumpster and watched the dark-haired bartender disappear into the club. The supernatural, even though he didn't get a garoul predator vibe from him was kind. His words sounded sincere and he truly sounded as if he cared about Cal's well-being. It made him relax somewhat and want to believe the bartender, but his paranoia over the fact that the attractive man's words could be nothing but a ploy to lead him into the clutches of the Hunters, his father, was still strong.

As much as he wanted to trust the hot bartender, he couldn't. Not yet, at least. So, while the man was inside, Cal belly crawled out from beneath the dumpster which was his minimal protection from hands that in the past wished to grab him.

He only spared a look over his shoulder toward the back door of the Witch's Brew before he ran toward the next closest building. All he wanted to do right at the moment was shift, call an Uber, and return to his newest grubby room to ponder what the hell happened tonight.

Travis carried the last three bags of trash out the back door. He didn't immediately toss them into the last dumpster which had space. No, instead he stopped before all three dumpsters and breathed in deep. The scent of the cat garoul was already faint enough to tell Travis that they were gone.

He could only hope they would take him up on his offer to return tomorrow night if for no other reason than to have a meal. Travis scanned the area behind the Brew. He didn't expect to see the bobcat, but that didn't stop him from looking.

Cal didn't relax until he closed the door to his latest crappy motel room. He didn't think the bartender would follow him, but that didn't stop Cal from feeling as if the supernatural would somehow grab him before he made it back to the dive of a motel room, he was currently calling home.

Why he ever thought to spy on the sexy bartender, he didn't know. Well, that was a lie. For the past couple weeks all he could think about was the dark haired supernatural he barely exchanged any words with while he was served at the bar in the Witch's Brew.

He should've known better than to cave in to his desire to see the man again. His mother taught him better; taught him there was always the possibility a supernatural could be a Hunter, too. However, he felt drawn to the bartender. Likely, it was just sexual attraction added on top of the fact the Witch's Brew had so many supernaturals in it when he was there on Valentine's Day. Still, as Cal stripped down and crawled under the ugly as hell bedspread and sheets, he couldn't stop hearing the bartender's sincere tone and words in his mind.

The supernatural seemed to really care about him. Cal had no doubt the man knew he was more than just a stray by the way the dark-haired man talked to him. The bartender never tried to drag him from his secure, well secure enough, hiding place beneath the center of the dumpster. That told Cal a lot. If the supernatural was a Hunter, he was sure the man wouldn't have been satisfied just leaving him in place where he hid.

Cal had already confirmed the Witch's Brew was frequented by supernaturals. The doorman wasn't a norm and neither was the sexy bartender he hoped to see again tonight. He did see him, but the sudden fear he felt caught him totally off guard. However, the bartender's words, the conversation since he obviously knew Cal wasn't *just* a cat filtered repeatedly across his mind. He did want to get to know the man better and as he drifted off to sleep, decided he would do just that by returning to the Witch's Brew the following night.

Travis had been distracted all day. His encounter with the small cat garoul after work wouldn't leave his thoughts. He finally gave up any attempt to get lost in one of his books and instead decided to clean. Travis' house was always spotless since he needed other things aside from reading and sex to fill up his sleepless hours. Cleaning was a mind-numbing task and was exactly what Travis needed at the moment.

Finally, four o'clock rolled around. Mikael and Adam didn't sleep either, but Travis would never visit them before four. It was a common courtesy in case they were busy traveling or doing something more intimate.

The alarm to the back door of the club would alert Mikael that someone entered. Travis shut it off. Of course, he could've shadow stepped directly into the club, but Travis thought of the alarm as a sort of doorbell for Mikael. He was only midway up the stairs when Adam greeted him from the second floor.

"You are here early, Travis." Adam smiled while he leaned on the rail. "Mikael didn't mention you were coming to hang out."

Travis gave Mikael's boyfriend a smile. Since the life drinkers didn't sleep, it was common for them to spend time together. However, courtesy usually dictated an invitation issued unless something was wrong.

"He was unaware I was stopping by," Travis admitted. "I hope I am not imposing."

"Not at all," Adam assured with a grin. "You are always welcome."

Adam turned and ran his security card over the sensor which would allow them access to Mikael's office and private apartment. Mikael stood in his open apartment door and smiled in greeting as they approached. Travis was one of the few Mikael allowed in his personal space and he was honored his longtime friend invited him in again.

"Is this a social visit or is something wrong?" Mikael tone was light once they were comfortably seated in the living room.

Travis easily read the concern in Mikael's eyes when he asked if something was wrong even though his tone of voice hadn't changed. They had been best friends for too many centuries for Travis not to recognize the shift in Mikael's gaze.

"A bit of both, maybe" Travis replied.

"You do not sound sure." Mikael raised a brow.

"Well, you both know I love socializing with you." Travis grinned. "In fact, I believe you both owe me a small fortune from the last time we played bridge."

Adam laughed. "I haven't had a few hundred years to perfect my game yet."

"Ain't that the truth," Travis easily agreed lightheartedly.

"But you're not here to collect." Mikael grinned. "I don't think you're here to play again, either."

"No, but now that you mentioned it." Travis stood and moved to the dining room table. "I can share my encounter from last night while I take more money from you both."

Travis took a seat at the table while Mikael chuckled and Adam groaned. By the time Mikael had retrieved the notebook they used to keep score of their marathon games, Adam had returned with the cards. Travis waited until they were all seated and the first hand was dealt before he informed them of the small cat garoul he'd encountered when he took out last night's trash.

"I think they were abandoned," Travis finished.

"Garouls rarely do that to their own," Mikael commented. "At least not to one who must be young if he is looking for a meal around dumpsters."

"So, he could've been kicked out of his family?" Adam asked with sincere concern.

"It has happened with garouls if they were troublesome before they were mature enough to leave on their own," Mikael answered. "The other possibility is they were adopted by a norm family and fled when they shifted for the first time at puberty."

All three life drinkers considered this possibility as Adam dealt another hand. It seemed all the men were lost in thought even though they were playing cards.

"What if...," Adam started, but appeared he didn't want to voice his thought. The frown on his face clearly indicated that was the case.

"If?" Travis prompted and met Adam's gaze.

"Maybe Hunters took out their family and the young garoul somehow managed to escape."

Silence settled around the table and their card game was forgotten. They had had to deal with Hunters seven months ago when their security employee Chris and his longtime boyfriend, Robert, had been swayed to believe the cultist bullshit the Hunters' spewed. However, as far as the employees at the Brew knew, the group which formed in Chicago had been disbanded.

"If that is the case," Mikael started and his frown matched his boyfriend's. "The Chicago sect is either still active or has reformed."

"That could explain why the bobtail garoul is foraging around dumpsters," Adam added.

"It would also explain why they are so skittish." Travis' frown joined his friends. "They would be able to sense if someone isn't a norm, but maybe haven't learned to discern what exactly they were sensing."

"Or, it wasn't a norm that took out their family," Adam said with a growl since he had plenty of experience being attacked by a non-norm right after he was turned.

"Any of these situations could be the case," Mikael pointed out. "But I am more inclines to think the Hunter aspect is more likely."

They had stopped playing cards mid hand when their conversation turned to speculation. Travis was glad he decided to visit Mikael and Adam. He was sure he would have eventually thought of the possibilities they offered. However, it was better for the small garoul he wished to help to have his friends offer them up before they occurred to him.

"I think your idea to coax the garoul out with the promise of a meal is a good one." Mikael gathered up the cards since they were obviously finished playing. "Perhaps, if you can befriend them, they will accept your help and ours by extension."

"That was my thinking, as well," Travis admitted. "I just hope they will take me up on my offer of a real meal and will return tonight."

"Speaking of meals…" Adam stood. "I'm hungry. Do you want to stay for steak, Travis?"

"Sure. I'd never turn down a good steak." Travis forced himself to grin even though his mind was still on the small bobcat garoul.

Chapter Five

Cal was nervous when he stepped out of the Uber in front of the same building from the night before. He had fallen asleep with thoughts of the bartender and woke up with the attractive man on his mind. Cal weighed the pros and cons of returning to The Witch's Brew in his feline form. Both swirled around in his head to the point he finally made a 'T' sheet to help him decide.

The cons consisted of everything Hunter related. His mother's death was at the top followed by the possibility of his directly underneath. Just seeing the two lines of Hunter related cons sparked his paranoia. However, the list of pros was much longer. Meeting more of the supernatural community was right at the top and underneath was listed how knowing more would offer better protection than hiding among the norms could ever provide. Of course, getting to know the sexy bartender, who seemed so sincere with wanting to help him, was on the list, as well. But it was the very last item he wrote and underlined several times on his pro list that decided his course of action.

Finally have a life.

It was that pro he repeated like a mantra to banish his paranoia when he turned the corner of the building closest to The Witch's Brew. He shifted a moment later with barely a thought.

It wasn't yet three a.m., so Cal casually padded toward the dumpster he'd hidden beneath last night. The stench of sour alcohol wasn't as strong. That told Cal the dumpsters had been emptied. For that he was grateful. There were worse smells he'd had to shower off in the past, but at least old booze wasn't too bad.

Cal slowed down as he approached the first dumpster and paused next to it to study the back door of the club. His vision was excellent in the low light provided by the string of blue neon lights that surrounded the roof of the club. The lights had been off last night, so he hadn't seen the box next to the door that looked like a keypad. He hadn't paid much attention last night to anything surrounding the back door.

Tonight however, he did. He easily spotted the plate that sat to the side of the back door. As if seeing the plate made the scent of chicken drift toward him. Like any feline, chicken was his second favorite food after fish. So, Cal wasn't surprised the bartender left him chicken instead of fish or cat food which was totally disgusting. The guy understanding he was a garoul was enough, Cal never expected to find cat food. The fact the sexy man left him chicken instead of fish said a lot about his knowledge of feline garouls. Or at least he understood how quickly fish could go bad even if the weather was cool.

Still, Cal didn't rush over to the food. He purposely missed dinner to see what the hot bartender would leave for him, so he was hungry. His paranoia made him cautious and as he creeped close to the dumpster, he paused before moving between them.

Cal strained to hear anything aside from the muted thump of bass coming from within the club. Slowly, Cal peeked his head out from between the two dumpsters in an attempt to hear better and scan the entire area behind the club. His night vision wasn't nearly as good tonight since the lights along the roof were off last night. However, the lights did brighten the area so he could see further even though his feline muted blue and grey vision didn't change.

He was satisfied he was alone behind The Witch's Brew, but he still hesitantly crept out from between the dumpsters. There were no shadows to hide in near the plate of chicken. That made him slightly nervous, so he belly crawled forward while occasionally swiveling his head from side to side to ensure he was still alone.

Cal knew better than to press himself against the wall of the club next to the plate of chicken. The last thing he would do was put his back to one of the directions along the back wall of the club. Instead, he remained hunched down in front of the plate and faced the back door. He would easily see any movement to his side from the corner of his eyes and have time to bolt.

He was half way through the surprisingly deliciously moist and tender chicken breast which had been cut into small pieces when the sound of the back door lock disengaging told him someone was coming out of the club. He didn't pause before leaping away and running between the dumpsters.

His heart was thumping so hard Cal thought it might beat straight out of his chest. Still, his racing heart didn't distract him from crawling under the middle dumpster to the same place he was safe from grabby hands.

"Shit."

Travis couldn't help cursing the moment he caught a flash of white, orange, and gray fur running for the dumpsters. He immediately stopped in the doorway to the club. The bobtail had been on his mind since first spotting the garoul. He had set the plate of chicken near the back door when he took a bathroom break earlier, but really didn't think the small garoul would make an appearance before the club closed for the night.

He must be hungrier than I thought.

Travis frowned and his heart ached even more. Thoughts of the bagged trash he held were forgotten when he looked down at the plate. Half of the chicken was gone and Travis hoped he could convince the bobtail to stick around long enough to finish the rest. Shit, he hoped the bobtail was still hiding under the dumpster and hadn't already run away.

Regardless, Travis remained frozen to the spot before he spoke. He had no doubt the small garoul would be able to hear him even with the loud club music filtering from behind him into the previously semi-silence surrounding the back of the building. If they were still here, of course.

"I'm sorry I scared you," Travis addressed the feline garoul sincerely. "I'm going to throw this away and won't be back out here until the club closes," Travis informed even if he was only talking to himself. "You should have plenty of time to finish."

Travis bent and picked up the plate before he approached the dumpsters. He set the plate down in front of the middle dumpster and used the toe of his boot to push it halfway under in hopes the garoul would feel safe enough to finish their meal. Travis cursed himself for not thinking of doing this in the first place.

"Throwing the trash in the dumpster, now," Travis told the bobtail so he wouldn't scare the garoul more than he already had when he opened the back door.

The bag of mostly empty beer bottles crashed loudly on the bottom of the dumpster to the right of the one he hoped the bobtail hid beneath. Travis didn't pause after the bang of shattering glass before he walked the several feet back to the club's door. However, he did stop halfway in the doorway and look back toward the dumpsters.

"I'm Travis, by the way. I'll keep putting food out for you and I want you to know you're safe here."

Travis didn't expect a reply or to see the bobtail come out from under the dumpster, if they were still even there at all.

Cal heard every word the bartender, Travis, said with the same sincerity from last night. Still, he waited until the supernatural disappeared through the club's back door before he used his paws to bat the plate back and forth until it was fully under the dumpster. His scare had caused him to lose his appetite even though the chicken had been delicious. However, he wanted Travis to think he'd finished the meal. So, he batted the remaining pieces of chicken off the plate before using his head to push the plate back to where the bartender originally placed it on the ground.

He debated sticking around to see the sexy bartender again. The music cutting off in the club indicated it was closing time. He had plenty of time to disappear back to the next building, shift, and call an Uber to take him back to his shitty motel. He just didn't want to when he could watch the hot bartender bring out the trash again. However, his current position wouldn't give him the full view he desired.

So, he slowly turned around under the dumpster and belly crawled until he could fully stand. The bartender he couldn't stop thinking about had to throw the trash away in the dumpster next to the one Cal hid beneath. Cal expected the man to use the same one when he brought out the rest of the trash.

Cal figured he had plenty of time to get in a position against the side of the dumpster the man used before the bartender made another appearance. He did just that. The lights along the roof went out and provided Cal more shadow to hide in as he crouched low to the ground. He peeked his head around the side of the dumpster just enough to have a clear line of sight of the path between the back door and cold dumpster along his flank.

Now, he just had to wait and ignore his racing heart that sounded loud in his ears.

Travis continued to berate himself for scaring the small garoul even though he hadn't thought the bobtail would have come back so early. He should have considered the garoul might have been hungry enough to return early since they had been scavenging around dumpsters for a meal.

Disgruntled with himself, Travis opened the back door slowly before he stepped outside. He had no idea if the small garoul was still around, but he was happy to spot the plate he'd moved was empty of the food he left.

Travis breathed in deeply. The scent of the garoul was still strong enough to assure him that the bobtail was either still here or had recently fled. Just the thought that the small garoul was still present after they finished eating gave Travis hope he was gaining the garoul's trust. That trust was the first step in helping them.

So, Travis moved slowly toward the dumpsters before he tossed the trash he held in. The crash of beer bottles breaking was expected, but Travis caught no sight of movement from the sound they made. After a pause, Travis returned inside to gather the remaining bags of trash.

Two trips later gave him the same result, but the scent of the garoul hadn't changed. They were still here and knowing that decided Travis' mind on what he would do next. He had no intention of catching the bobtail, but he did want to see more than the white, orange, and grey fur and the rear end of them. So, he returned inside the club and with barely a thought shadow stepped behind the dumpsters. However even remaining incorporeal, he wasn't totally silent. He had to breathe after all.

He was more than sure the feline garoul's sensitive hearing would detect every breath he took, so he focused his attention on the bottom of the dumpsters. Still, his expectation the garoul wouldn't come out was shattered when he caught a flash of fur off to his side.

The bobtail had already left their secure hiding place under the dumpster and currently bolted away in the direction of the building closest to The Witch's Brew. However, half way there the small feline garoul stopped and looked back over its shoulder. It was this pause in flight that gave Travis his first good look at the bobtail. They were primarily white. Black and grey stripes of a tabby cat covered their shoulders and in the other direction to cover their head down to their nose. Two of their legs, a front and back, were sporadically mottled in orange and the color appeared to disappear under their belly. This wasn't just a bobtail. It was a beautiful calico bobtail.

Travis was still invisible in the shadows, but the small garoul fleeing was enough to let him know he'd been detected. The bobtail pausing in their flight gave Travis hope that this wouldn't be the last time they interacted with one another. He still didn't reveal himself, though, nor did he follow when the garoul turned and ran toward the other building.

The weekend came and went. In fact, it had almost been two weeks since his last encounter with the hot bartender. Cal had switched shithole hotels three times since then, but not because he felt the bartender, Travis, was following him. No, it was pure habit by this point not to stay in one place for too long.

He already knew Travis wasn't a norm even if he didn't know what the man actually was. He at least knew he wasn't a norm. Still, he didn't know enough about the supernatural community to know which non-norms had the ability to be invisible.

His education where the other supernaturals were concerned was severely lacking since his mother focused more on keeping them alive than anything else. Cal was sure he wouldn't even have been taught that much if they had been able to remain hidden amongst norms and not crossed paths with any supernaturals at all. He understood his mother's desire to keep him sheltered from the supernatural community, but doing so had only made life more difficult since her death.

It was just thinking of his lack of education that made Cal angry. Yes, he understood his mother's motivation for trying to hide them in plain sight amongst the norms, but that didn't stop him from being angry with her. Telling him to never stay in one motel for too long, never trust anyone, and stay on the move just wasn't enough. He understood her lessons were meant to keep him alive, but he was tired. Twenty-four years old and he was tired. So, fucking tired.

Not running could mean his death if his father or any other Hunters found him. Cal was more than aware of this. However, crossing paths with several supernaturals while he worked in the coffee shop was enough to make him inquire about clubs. Hearing about The Witch's Brew from so many of them was the only reason he chanced visiting the club over a month ago. He was more than glad he had, even though his paranoia to check it out almost got the better of him.

Tonight was Saturday, though. The Witch's Brew should be busy since it was the weekend. Granted, it likely wouldn't be as packed as Valentine's Day, but that was okay. Cal felt safer when there was a crowd, especially if said crowd included a lot of norms. So, with a last look in the bathroom mirror he ordered an Uber to take him to The Witch's Brew.

Travis was as busy as any other Saturday night. However, he was working on autopilot. Autopilot had been his mode for the last two weeks. He was too pissed off at himself and too concerned over the small garoul he'd only seen twice out by the dumpsters. He was pissed off because he knew it was his fault the garoul hadn't returned. He never should've hid in the shadows when he was sure the little garoul would scent or hear his presence. Travis was just too curious for his own good to catch sight of them. Of course, the concern that was practically eating him alive was because every plate of food he'd left out since that night remained untouched.

"A rum and Coke, Jack and Coke, and three lemon drop shots," Cat's order from where she stood at the end of the bar shook Travis from his guilty thoughts about the small garoul.

Travis mixed the drinks and set them on her tray before he turned away to make the shots. No sooner did he add them to the tray did Cat grabbed his wrist. He raised a questioning brow at her.

"You okay? You seem distracted," she asked with clear concern in her gaze.

This wasn't the first time one of his friends asked him that question and he loved them for worrying about him. Still, he gave her the same response he'd been spewing the last couple of weeks.

"I'm good." Travis smiled even though Cat frowned at his reply.

Just like every time before when he answered, she didn't say anything else before she lifted her tray and disappeared into the crowd to deliver the drinks. Only Mikael and Adam were aware of the true depth of his concern over the small, apparently homeless, garoul. However, even they agreed there wasn't anything he could do about the situation.

Travis gave himself a mental shake and forced himself to focus on the patrons that lined his bar. The bar was one to two people deep in some places, so Travis started with his closest customer and took their drink order to fill.

The Witch's Brew was as busy as Cal expected it to be, but not as busy as Valentine's Day. He expected this as well. Still, he couldn't decide if not sensing so many supernaturals compared to the last time he was here was a good thing or not.

The large doorman was the same employee and sat in the same place as last time. He was a garoul of some sort, a possible predator of some sort. The vibe he got from the huge man was confusing. Cal felt the garoul was big; most were compared to him, but what he sensed as far as if the man was a predator or not was confusing.

So, he forced thoughts of the doorman garoul out of his mind after he entered the club.

Cal moved through the crowd toward Travis' bar and sensed two more garouls along the way. They were *definitely* predators. He paused to see if he could locate them. But, before he could, a stronger awareness of a non-norm assaulted him. Cal didn't need to search the crowd to locate the supernatural. A large muscular man wearing a bright neon yellow T-shirt just like the doorman's stopped walking only a few feet away from him. This man wasn't a garoul, but something else. Cal gave the supernatural a wide berth and barely resisted looking over his shoulder while he moved through the crowd to get closer to the short end of the bar where Travis was working.

There were enough club goers between Cal and Travis when he wedged himself between the wall and the short end of the bar the he had plenty of time to watch the sexy bartender work. He enjoyed watching Travis work without the man realizing he was being scrutinized. Although, at the rate the man was serving the club's customers, Cal wouldn't have long to enjoy the view. Still, that didn't mean Cal wouldn't absorb every second so he could enjoy the memory later.

Finally, Travis reached the last two customers closest to him. Cal couldn't help the small smile which spread his lips when Travis glanced his way. Travis returned his smile. Well, that wasn't totally true since Travis had already been smiling at his other customers before he glanced in Cal's direction. Still, Cal pretended that smile was just for him. He couldn't help but fantasize that was true, especially after hearing how sincere Travis was in his attempt to help him while he was in his feline form.

Cal observed Travis set down the drinks in front of the people to the side of him. Travis turned away from his last customers and moved the two steps it took to put himself in front of Cal.

"Hey beautiful. A water?"

Cal blinked in surprise at not only being called beautiful again by Travis, but at the man actually remembering what he'd ordered a month ago. All he could manage was a nod to confirm that was what he wanted.

Chapter Six

Travis caught sight of the pretty blonde from a month ago as he worked his way down the bar filling drink orders. The guy was just as beautiful as he remembered which was saying a lot considering Travis barely remembered his regulars let alone his random casual hookups. Not that this pretty man had been a hookup. However, maybe it was the soft looking curly blonde hair that reached the collar of his black T-shirt or the man's light eyes that had to be either gray or blue that made Travis remember him. Travis didn't know. He really didn't care why his one interaction with the garoul made such an impression on him, either.

"Here you go." Travis set down a bottle of water in front of the pretty man before he twisted the top off. "You're not going to disappear into the shadows again, are you?"

The smile Travis leveled on him was flirty and Cal couldn't help but smile in return. Just the fact that Travis not only remembered he ordered a water last time, but also remembered he tried to blend into the wall when there wasn't any room to stand at the bar was impressive.

"I'm sure I'm good here, tonight," Cal replied boldly even though he didn't feel so bold.

"Good." Travis continued to smile.

He was more than pleased the beautiful blonde would stay leaning against the bar. The crowd tonight was typical, but the spot the guy occupied was practically in the corner of the bar and Travis was sure no one would try to move him from his position in order to get a drink.

"What's your name, pretty?" Travis flirted and needed to know since he wanted to address him by something other than 'beautiful' or 'pretty'. Not that those weren't totally appropriate descriptions of the man.

"Calvin," Cal replied and almost said something along the lines of 'and you're Travis' but he caught himself just in time. "You are?" Cal forced himself to ask so he wouldn't slip up at some point.

"Travis." He held out his hand to shake. Travis would've sworn he felt a spark of electricity between them when their palms touched if he believed in such a thing.

"Nice to meet you, Travis." Cal couldn't stop smiling at the sexy as hell bartender, even though he knew it was a dangerous thing to even consider hooking up with the man regardless of how long it had been since he'd had sex.

"Pleasure meeting you, Calvin." Travis gave him a wink and he was about to speak again before he was interrupted.

"Travis, I have an order," Cat yelled down the bar to him.

Travis looked over his shoulder to acknowledge Cat before he turned back to Calvin. "Are you going to be here for a while or disappear into the herd again?"

Travis' question was lighthearted, but Cal wasn't sure how he should answer. As much as his body craved the touch of another, not even sexually, but just the touch, he wasn't sure if staying until closing time again was a good thing. The fact that Travis seemed to want him to stick around, seemed interested enough to even ask, made Cal even more indecisive.

So, Cal gave the only answer he could. "I haven't decided yet."

Travis smiled. He liked Calvin's honesty. It said a lot about the guy's character. The garoul's character. Calvin wasn't just out for a quick hookup and that pleased Travis immensely for some reason.

"Fair enough." Travis gave the pretty blonde a nod. "At least say goodbye if you decide to leave."

Cal grinned. "I can do that."

"Travis!"

"You better get back to work." Cal nodded toward the blonde-haired waitress who stood at the opposite end of the bar and was clearly waiting for Travis to fill her drink orders.

Travis thumped his fist on the bar twice in front of Cal before he spoke, "guess I better."

With that, Cal watched Travis turn and walk toward the waitress. Cal couldn't help but appreciate the view. Travis only spent a moment with her before turning back to the bar and mixing drinks. He couldn't take his gaze away from the man. Every flex of Travis' forearm and what Cal could see of his biceps while the sexy as fuck bartender mixed drinks made Cal's mouth water. Just watching the supernatural work also stroked Cal's libido.

Being sexually attracted to anyone was a dangerous thing for Cal. He took care of his needs with his hand or with random pickups with norms, usually in dingy dark alleys, but never with another supernatural. His mother's paranoia and the fear she imbued in him was strong, so every sexual experience in his life was over far too quickly for it to be more than just a quick release.

However, the sincerity of Travis' concern for him while he was shifted and his attraction to the supernatural made the ingrained mistrust his mother instilled in him to feel muted. Watching Travis work after getting to know the supernatural's compassion when he was in his animal form only further smothered his mother's warnings.

Travis filled Cat's drink order and felt no shame when he looked down the bar and into the corner where Calvin stood before he started filling other patrons' orders. The crowd was enough Travis served one to two deep as he worked his way down the bar. By the time he reached Calvin and had been ready to ask if he wanted another water, there was no need. Calvin was barely halfway through the bottle Travis had originally served him. As much as he wanted to stop in front of the adorable man again, there was no reason to do so when other customers wanted refills. Still, that didn't stop Travis from smiling at Calvin and even shooting him another wink.

Cal wasn't surprised to be on the receiving end of Travis' smile. He wasn't even surprised when the man winked at him. In fact, the open flirtation sent warmth through him. Travis had flirted with him the same way on Valentine's Day, but he hadn't had the same reaction even though he was sexually attracted to the supernatural. He was sure what he felt had everything to do with the compassion Travis showed him while he was in his feline form. Travis had no reason to be concerned about a *stray* even if the supernatural realized he wasn't a norm and that made all the difference now.

He was sure it was that unexpected caring for another supernatural which not only made Travis more attractive, on the mental front, but also made Cal less wary of him. Still, Cal wasn't sure if he should stick around until the club closed. He wanted to, but not trusting anyone was ingrained in him so deeply he wasn't sure he'd be able to whether they were a supernatural or norm.

Travis made his way down the bar again and set another bottle of water in front of Calvin. He didn't twist the top off of it and ignored the blonde's startled reaction to his presence.

"You look lost in your thoughts." Travis smiled when Cal's pale eyes focused on him.

Cal wasn't surprised by the concern he heard in Travis' question. However, he wasn't happy to be caught off guard lost in thought. Still, that didn't stop the almost shy smile that spread his lips.

"I was," Cal replied to Travis' comment.

"Are you okay?"

"Not sure," Cal answered Travis' question and tried not to frown. He wasn't sure which one of them was more surprised by his honesty.

Travis wasn't expecting Calvin to say anything other than 'I'm fine' or 'I'm good' so when the beautiful man answered otherwise, it caught him off guard. He wasn't sure how to answer so instead, he leaned forward and folded his arms on top of the bar in front of Calvin.

Travis was well aware the beautiful blonde was a garoul, but his current position put him close enough to actually scent the man. What he smelled caught him so off guard that he hadn't even settled his weight fully on his folded arms before he pulled back and stood upright.

The pretty man who stood across the bar from him smelled just like the bobtail garoul he'd been trying to befriend outside the back of the club. Travis made sure his friendly and flirty expression didn't change while he looked Calvin over again. The blonde didn't look homeless. He wasn't skin and bones and his clothes weren't what were typically dirty and threadbare.

Calvin's scent was unmistakable from what he smelled from the garoul behind the club. However, before he could put the few pieces of the puzzle that were the beautiful blonde together, the house lights came on and The Witch's Brew DJ called for last call.

"You better serve the horde," Cal said with a chuckle and nod toward where several people were lined up at the bar.

"You'll be here when I'm done?" Travis couldn't help but ask. It was beyond him how he even managed to get his question out once the bar lights were on and he could see the pale blue eyes that met his.

Cal just offered Travis a shrug in reply to his question. He wanted to stay. Wanted to talk to Travis more and wanted to give into his attraction. However, his mother's voice in his head prevented him from doing so.

Travis was serving his last few customers and not paying any attention to Cal. It was the perfect opportunity to slip away from the bar and blend in with the crowd that was shuffling out the door.

Travis sat down the last drinks for the diehards that needed to squeeze in one more before they were kicked out. He paid no mind to them guzzling down their alcohol. Instead, he turned toward the short side of his bar, more specifically toward the corner where the garoul's whose trust he had been trying to gain stood. The pretty man was gone and somehow Travis wasn't too surprised. Disappointed, yes, surprised, no.

He released a deep sigh and stared at the empty space where Calvin had previously stood. At least now he had a name to go with the small garoul who he had seen a few times by the club's dumpsters. Recognizing the calico bobtail in his human form drinking water across the bar from him was more than unexpected.

The man didn't seem nearly as skittish in his human form as he had in his feline one, but Travis thought he understood why. Calvin likely could defend himself better in his human form than his garoul one since small garouls could easily be prey for those who were larger.

Calvin hadn't returned to the dumpsters since Travis hid in the shadows to get a better look at him. After seeing the way the beautiful blonde was dressed in the club, Travis couldn't help but question why he was hanging around the dumpsters behind the Brew at all. Calvin's clothes weren't those of someone who was homeless. They weren't those which would warrant scavenging meals from dumpsters, either. Just knowing this now, confused Travis, but Calvin had to have a reason.

For the last two weeks, Travis had set out a plate of chicken in hopes the bobtail garoul, who he thought was homeless, would return. He had no doubt he'd scared off the small garoul after their last encounter, but he still put the food out. He decided meeting Calvin again in the club wasn't going to stop his now nightly ritual of putting food out. It was more than obvious to Travis that Calvin was more comfortable in his animal form even though he was practically defenseless against larger garouls.

Travis also had no doubt that Calvin knew who he was when he came into the club tonight. But, just because Calvin knew this, didn't mean the pretty garoul would implicitly trust him. All Travis could do was keep trying to build on that trust, whether that meant putting chicken on a plate or speaking to the pretty man if he came into the Brew. Travis would do it because he was more than sure Calvin needed the community and the family, which Travis called home.

Cal had wanted to stay the last time he went to The Witch's Brew. Just the few words he'd exchanged with Travis made him want to hear more of the sexy bartender's deep soothing voice. Cal didn't even try to kid himself over his attraction for the supernatural. Still, that attraction which only increased the last time he was in the man's presence wasn't enough to make him stay when The Witch's Brew closed. He wanted to stay, but just couldn't.

That was almost a week ago. A very long week because all he could think about was Travis and seeing him again. Cal finally caved into his desire to see Travis once more and went back to The Witch's Brew.

Being dropped off by an Uber driver, walking around the side of the building, and shifting almost felt like a habit since he'd done it a few times already. It was almost three a.m. when Cal crept under the middle dumpster he'd used as a hiding place before. What Cal hadn't expected was the scent of chicken coming from the just as unexpected plate that sat in front of the dumpster he preferred to hide under.

The chicken wasn't old. It was fresh which told him Travis had been putting food out for him even though he hadn't been back for over a month. Warmth once more flooded Cal's chest. He wasn't hungry, but still batted the plate with his paws until it settled near him under the dumpster. Cal had just finished using his paws to swat the pieces of cut up chicken off the plate when the clubs music cut off.

The lights along the roof shut off moments later. Cal froze. He didn't realize he'd arrived so close to closing time, but then realized it was a Sunday so it likely didn't take the club as long to close. Still, he wanted to make sure the plate was back in its original position before Travis came out the back door.

Well, if wanting were wishes, beggars would all be rich. Cal had only batted the plate four times in an effort to move it from beneath the dumpster before the back door opened. He froze once again at the sound.

Every night Travis took out the clubs trash his gaze immediately looked at the plate of food he left out for the small garoul. The same small garoul he now knew to be the beautiful man named Calvin. Since the night he got Calvin's name, the food on the plate remained untouched. That still didn't deter him from putting fresh chicken out every night close to closing time in hopes of another encounter. So, seeing the half empty plate sticking halfway out from under the dumpster caused him to pause.

Travis breathed in deeply. The scent he now knew belonged to Calvin was strong. So strong that he had no doubt the small garoul was still present. Travis wanted to call out to Calvin, but decided against doing so until after he finished bringing out the night's trash.

He gave one more glance at the near empty plate that was further underneath the dumpster than where he had left it before he threw the trash into the dumpster and returned to the bar.

Cal laid belly down, his front paws on each side of the plate that was still almost under the dumpster. He watched Travis and didn't miss the man's slow movements to throw the club trash in the dumpster.

Cal expected Travis to say something since he had no doubt the supernatural was aware of his presence. Travis said nothing, though, and Cal wasn't sure what to make of the man's silence. Travis not talking to him as he had before made Cal nervous; not nervous enough to flee, but nervous just the same.

All he could do was wait, watch, and hope Travis would say something when he brought out the rest of the trash.

Travis gave no thought to the last three bags of trash he brought out of the back door of the club. He gave no thought to tossing them into the dumpster, either. Calvin's scent was still strong, so he knew the garoul was still hiding around the dumpsters.

It was knowing that, knowing Calvin in his garoul form was close, which had him sitting on the small step near the back door. Travis lowered himself down to the cold concrete slowly. He rested his arms on his bent knees and waited. He didn't think Calvin would come out of his hiding place under the dumpster, but Travis didn't sleep so he had all the time in the world to wait for him to come out.

Cal watched Travis from his hidden spot. The sexy supernatural just sat on the ground, totally relaxed, with his back toward the door. Travis hadn't tried to talk to him, hadn't said a word, and Cal wasn't sure what to make of the supernatural's behavior.

By Cal's calculation, close to an hour passed by and Travis did nothing. It seemed as if Travis was purposely waiting for him to do something. Something stupid, like reveal himself. He could easily back out of his hiding spot, but there was nowhere Travis wouldn't see him take off. Seeing him flee wasn't too much of a worry to Cal, but not knowing what kind of supernatural

Travis was, aside from not being a garoul, and what abilities he might possess made Cal stay exactly where he was.

Playing a waiting game didn't bother Travis at all. He was perfectly content to sit on the back stoop of The Witch's Brew.

Chapter Seven

Cal was sure another hour had passed, making it two hours now after the club closed. Travis still sat casually with his forearms hanging over his bent knees. He expected the bartender to talk to him as he had the last few times he'd hidden under The Witch's Brew dumpsters. Cal could admit he was disappointed the supernatural remained silent.

It crossed Cal's mind that Travis was waiting for him to make an appearance. However, as much as he wanted to believe Travis was trustworthy, Cal was still trepidatious when it came to the other supernatural. Still, the silence between them was getting on Cal's nerves and he had the sense he'd have to be the one to break it.

"Meow." Cal exhaled quietly.

"So, you are still here," Travis said and couldn't help smiling. "I was starting to think I was sitting here by myself."

Cal remained quiet for several more minutes before acknowledging Travis with another soft meow.

"You know you can come out from under there, right?" Travis whispered softly in a lighthearted tone. It took everything he had not to call the garoul out, say his name, but he knew to do so would shatter any trust he'd already built.

Cal exhaled another quiet meow and belly crawled toward the front of the dumpster where the empty plate still rested. From his current position, Cal could see Travis' body. His line of sight ended at Travis' chest. He wanted, no desired, to see the supernatural's face so he belly crawled toward him a few more inches.

Travis smiled when he saw Calvin's black and gray tabby pattern on white appear from under the dumpster. There wasn't much light behind The Witch's Brew, but Travis really didn't need light to see. Seeing in the dark was only one benefit of a life drinker. However, he was pleased to see what little light there was reflecting off Calvin's eyes.

"There you are." Travis continued to smile. "You are safe here. Safe at The Witch's Brew," Travis repeated what he'd told Calvin before. "You're safe with me."

Cal was hesitant. Everything his mother taught him made his knee-jerk reaction not to trust anyone make an appearance. Still, Travis' sincere words and gaze made him think there was something about Travis and they made all the barriers his mother built crack. They didn't crumble, but they cracked and that crack dared Cal to be reckless.

Slowly, he belly crawled from beneath the dumpster until his body fully cleared the heavy metal that was his protection.

Travis didn't move. Not that he had moved in the last two hours. However, seeing Calvin's calico bobtail feline form finally creep out from under the dumpster made Travis want to pick him up and hold him to show him that he wasn't alone in the world.

Cal was more than nervous as his tail end was the only part of his body that still connected with the safety of his hiding spot under the dumpster. He wanted to trust Travis, but was still leery. He felt skittish, so he paced, rubbed himself, along the side of the dumpster even though the metal was filthy. Cal was more than sure he could flee and escape if Travis made any move to grab him.

Travis still didn't move a muscle. He was a life drinker, so he was more than experienced in staying still and his patience was endless. He just watched Calvin hesitantly pace back and forth, remaining close to the dumpster. It broke his heart all over again that this beautiful blonde appeared so afraid of another from their supernatural community.

"You really are beautiful." Travis paused to see what Calvin would do

Cal let Travis' deep soothing voice caress him. Travis' words weren't ones he hadn't heard the man speak before, but he couldn't deny the warmth that flooded him at hearing them again. That warmth was likely to blame for Cal moving away from the safety of the dumpsters and approaching Travis.

Travis hid his surprise when Calvin slowly moved away from the dumpsters. The feline garoul which was the beautiful blonde Travis had met in the bar, slowly and cautiously crossed the distance between them. He wanted to address the calico bobtail by his name, the name the pretty man gave him when they interacted across the bar, but something deep inside told Travis that would be a mistake. So as much as Travis wanted to let Calvin know he knew who he really was, he went with his gut not to do so. Travis didn't want Calvin to bolt again, so he said nothing and watched the bobtail.

Travis not moving gave Cal more courage. Travis' caring words played a part in pushing his paranoia to the back of his mind, as well. Cal had no doubt he could run away if Travis made a move to grab him. He also had no doubt if Travis did grab him, he could use his claws to shred the supernatural in an attempt to get free. However, Cal didn't think that would be needed where Travis was concerned.

So, slowly he paced between Travis and the dumpster. Every lap brought him closer to Travis. The supernatural didn't move, didn't even flinch, and Cal was reassured Travis was as sincere as every word he spoke.

Travis kept his serene smile on his lips while he watched Calvin cautiously approach. He wasn't surprised by Calvin's hesitant pacing approach. Travis had already determined the garoul wasn't familiar enough with the supernatural community to discern what he was. He had no doubt Calvin realized he wasn't a norm, but he could only hope that Calvin realized he wanted nothing more than to help.

He maintained eye contact with Calvin's incredible golden eyes. Travis had no doubt that had the club's roof lights still been on, he'd see nothing but a reflection gleam from the small garoul's eyes. However, the club lights were off and Travis' night vision was superb so he had no problem seeing the golden beauty of Calvin's eyes.

Calvin felt encouraged by the fact Travis had still not moved. In fact, the supernatural was practically statue still, aside from his eyes which tracked every movement Cal made. He wasn't sure if it was Travis' stillness or remembering how sincere the supernatural sounded when he offered to help Cal that made him creep closer. He was within arm's reach of Travis and the man remained frozen in place. Cal's heart was thumping so hard he not only felt it trying to explode from his chest, but he felt as if his ears might explode from the loud beat. Still, that didn't stop him from stepping closer.

Travis still did nothing more than watch Calvin. He wanted to reach out and run his hand along the soft looking fur which covered Calvin's back. But, he was sure that would not only startle the sexy garoul, but cause him to flee. So, as he had been doing for the last two hours, Travis didn't move a muscle as Calvin inched closer. Travis' breath hitched when Calvin hesitantly rubbed his body against his booted foot.

It took every ounce of Cal's courage to make contact with Travis. He never looked away from the hot bartender who sat with his arms still draped over his bent knees and could have easily touched him when he rubbed his flank against Travis' black boot. Cal was more than prepared to leap away if Travis moved, but the supernatural didn't.

Travis' lack of movement allowed Cal to relax. He never looked away from the pale eyes that followed his every move while he slid his body against the man's legs. Cal did it one direction, then the other. The purr that escaped his throat couldn't be helped. This was the first time he'd made contact with anyone while in his garoul form since Abe.

"I want to pet you. Will you let me?" Travis whispered and hated that Calvin startled and leapt away.

Cal reacted instinctively when Travis spoke. He leapt out of reach, but didn't bolt. He didn't fear Travis even though he knew his mother would beat him senseless for feeling this way. Travis asking to pet him and not moving when he jumped away only built on the trust he felt toward the supernatural even though he wasn't sure what the man actually *was*.

Travis sat patiently in the same position he'd been in for over two and half hours. He wasn't uncomfortable. Staying still to gain Calvin's trust was his only thought. He regretted speaking, but scaring Calvin by speaking was better than the small garoul thinking he was being attacked by Travis attempting to touch him. Now at least, Calvin was aware of what he wanted to do. He made sure Calvin was in total control of the situation and had no doubt the decision being fully left up to Calvin would only reinforce the trust he was trying to build.

Cal stood out of Travis' reach for several minutes. The sexy bartender hadn't moved an inch. He still sat on the concrete in front of the club's back door. Travis' arms still rested relaxingly on his bent knees. The supernatural looked harmless, but Cal was well aware that a supernatural was anything but harmless. However, Travis appeared so and the man had been nothing but sincere with his concern to help him.

Travis could see the indecision in Calvin's eyes. Garoul or not, the indecision was clear as day nonetheless. Once again, Travis regretted saying anything to cause Calvin to put distance between them. That moment was fleeting even though Calvin still stood out of reach and stared at him warily.

"I won't hurt you," Travis whispered again. "Come here."

Travis moved his arm slowly to stretch it out and offer his palm up to Calvin. He was still leery of revealing he knew who Calvin was because the small garoul obviously had a valid reason for why he felt he needed to remain hidden from their community.

Calvin had put enough distance between them he felt safe if the bartender attempted to grab him. However,

Travis didn't do anything other than hold out his hand. The rest of the man's body still remained statue still. So, he crept closer, close enough to feel Travis' hand on his head before he even considered the pros and cons of doing so.

The sudden heat of Travis' palm resting on his head and the gentle curl of the bartender's fingers to scratch behind his ears caused him to purr loudly. Not only purr, but arch his back in pure pleasure. Cal hadn't been caressed this way since Abe and he had no idea how much he had missed the sensation.

Travis scratched behind Calvin's ears while he rested his palm on Calvin's head. The purrs that reached his ears was almost as gratifying as the vibration from the noise he could feel beneath his palm. The more he scratched behind Calvin's ears, the more the small garoul pressed into his hand and rubbed against his leg. It was more than obvious that Calvin hadn't had any affection, in either form, in a long time. That realization totally shifted Travis' desire to hook up with the beautiful blonde to something else.

"Meow." Cal pushed harder into Travis' hand.

Every lesson his mother taught him and every instinctual pang of paranoia seemed to melt away under Travis' hand. Somewhere in the back of Cal's mind, he knew feeling this way and trusting someone he didn't know, a supernatural of all things, was dangerous. His mother didn't trust norms, but she distrusted non-norms even more. Still, that didn't stop him from pressing more firmly into Travis' hand which was giving him so much pleasure just by scratching behind his ears.

Travis couldn't help but smile at feeling the vibration of Cal's purr through the palm of his hand. His enhanced hearing heard Calvin's purr as if the small garoul were right next to his ear. There was something vastly satisfying and relaxing from feeling Calvin's pleasure from his touch.

Cal's purr was loud to him in the silence behind The Witches Brew. Travis' palm smoothing the hairs down along his back or his fingers scratching his cheeks or up his neck to his chin was heavenly. So heavenly, Cal couldn't help but purr. He almost forgot where he was and who he was with when memories of Abe flooded his mind. Cal missed the old blind man dearly and not just because Cal felt safe and taken care of while living with Abe. He did miss that, but he missed moments like this when Abe would just let his feline be a cat and have no worries in the world.

Cal had no idea how long he rubbed against Travis' legs and allowed the supernatural to pet him. However, the sky was brightening with pale shades of morning and Cal could hear the beginning of rush-hour traffic steadily picking up. It was time to go.

When Calvin started to move away, Travis didn't attempt to stop him. He was happy, but more relieved Calvin had trusted him enough to come so close. There was no doubt in Travis' mind that this was a big step for the skittish garoul, so Travis decided to make what happened tonight part of his daily routine and return after closing time. Hopefully, he could encourage Calvin's trust in him to the point the pretty blonde would accept his help.

Cal stopped near the far dumpster and looked over his shoulder at Travis. He needed to shift, but the shadows near the closest building where he usually shifted were not to be found in the morning light. Cal had no desire to get closer to the busy morning traffic, either. So, he gave Travis a meow and moved his head in a nod toward the back door of The Witches Brew. Thankfully, Travis understood his message.

Travis slowly and smoothly stood. It was clear Calvin wanted privacy to shift and Travis understood garouls usually preferred it that way. So, he punched in the security code for the door and didn't speak until he was halfway back into the club.

"Thank you for tonight." Travis smiled. "I hope to see you again tonight after closing time."

Cal only replied with another soft meow before Travis disappeared into the club. Once the gorgeous man was out of sight, Cal shifted and called an Uber to take him back to his shithole of a motel.

This became their routine for the next two weeks and Cal was enjoying the time he spent with Travis while in this form until Travis broke his pleasure with a new question one night.

"Do you want to come home with me?"

Cal froze beneath Travis' hand. He stopped purring and pressing his body against Travis' bent leg. He looked up and met Travis' eyes that appeared a pale gray. Cal saw nothing but a true offer to take care of him. He was more than sure the sexy supernatural bartender only wanted to help him by giving him some place to stay for the night. Cal didn't need somewhere to stay, but the idea of staying with Travis was almost too strong to resist.

"You don't have to shift, unless it's close to being dangerous for you," Travis said softly. "Let me take you home and give you a good night of sleep. I'll bring you back in the morning. I promise."

Cal thought of the crappy hotel room he was staying in and didn't look forward to returning to that shithole. Travis offering to take him home was appealing, even more so, because the supernatural said he didn't need to shift. So, Cal decided to take the chance, as reckless as it was, and accept the sexy bartender's invitation. Slowly, Cal moved alongside Travis' body until he could creep under Travis' arm, into his lap, and press his head under Travis' chin.

To say that Travis was surprised Calvin not only accepted his offer to go home with him, but also climbed into his lap would have been an understatement. However, he didn't immediately stand to take them home. Instead, he slowly moved his arm until his hand was close enough to caress Calvin soft fur again.

"I'm going to pet you again," Travis whispered softly like every time before he actually touched Calvin.

Cal wanted to feel Travis' warm hand on him again, so he tilted his head and pushed up into Travis' palm to give the supernatural permission as he had done every time in the past. Travis started between his ears and dragged his hand down Cal's back. Cal couldn't help but arch into the touch.

Travis continued to pet Calvin for a good five minutes before he spoke again. "I'm going to pick you up now," Travis warned and was given a meow that he took for permission to do so. He cupped his hand under Calvin's belly and pressed the pretty bobtail to his chest before he used his other hand and legs to push himself to his feet. He didn't hesitate to punch in the door code and enter the bar.

"I'm going to take us home now," Travis told Calvin as he stepped into a shadowed spot behind the stairs. Calvin was thankfully small enough Travis could shadows step with him. So, with a thought of his dark bathroom at home, he did just that.

Cal wasn't sure what the hell just happened. One moment they were standing inside The Witch's Brew and the next they appeared to be in a dark bathroom. He was only able to discern it was a bathroom because the thin line of light under the closed door was just enough for him to see. Needless to say, he freaked the hell out.

Travis' hands which had felt so comforting and gentle now felt like a vice grip trapping him against the man's chest. Cal's claws came out and instinctively he twisted his body in an effort to get free. The fact that Travis didn't try to stop him didn't even register in his panicked mind.

His claws connected with the tile floor and he scrambled to gain purchase. Once he had, he bolted toward the first hiding place he could find. The bathroom wasn't very large and the wicker hamper wasn't a very good hiding place. Still, he squeezed his body behind it and it would just have to do until Travis opened the door.

"Fuck!" Travis spat out and his curse had nothing to do with Calvin's claws had left deep scratches on his chest.

His gaze followed Calvin's flight from his hold. He didn't even think about how Calvin would react to his shadow stepping. Thoughts of what Calvin did or didn't know about the supernatural community and what those who lived within it could do, never crossed his mind before he brought them both home to his house. Travis should have known better after Calvin's reaction to him staying in the shadows to see more of him in his animal form.

"I'm sorry," Travis said sincerely and only turned sideways enough to see where Calvin bolted in order to find a safe hiding place. "I should have warned you about shadow stepping."

Travis could easily see where Calvin had squeezed himself behind the hamper. He had no intention of approaching Calvin or trying to pull him from his hiding place. Still, his apology only garnered a low warning growl from Calvin.

Cal couldn't stop his thumping panicked heart. As much as Travis sounded totally sincere with his apology, Cal's paranoia for being caught with no escape flooded him so strongly his entire body was shaking. All he could do was rumble a warning toward what could be a threat. He tried to remind himself Travis hadn't done anything to warrant his sudden fear, panic, and paranoia. It didn't work. His mother's voice was too damn strong in his mind. All he could do was protect himself defensively by hiding and issuing his warning.

"I didn't mean to scare you."

Travis turned fully around to face his hamper. He squatted down, but didn't move closer. The urge to reassure Calvin by picking him up was even stronger, but Travis resisted.

Cal didn't move, but instead continued to growl low in warning when Travis squatted down. Travis only remained squatted for a moment and a hiss escaped Cal's throat when Travis stood. He watched the sexy bartender slowly back away toward the door before Travis opened it. Cal blinked several times to adjust his eyes to the morning sunshine which suddenly filled the bathroom around Travis' body.

He weighed his chances of escape. There wasn't much space around the supernatural's legs, but if he remained in the bathroom Travis could trap him by closing the door. If that happened, Cal would have no choice but to shift in order to escape.

What would I do then? Cal couldn't help but think.

Travis and he were almost the same height, but the bartender had more muscle. That added to the fact Calvin had no idea what Travis was other than not being a garoul gave him no idea of the man's strength. Plus, he also had no idea where he was. Those thoughts caused Calvin to decide to stay put for the moment and deal with the possibility of Travis trapping him in the bathroom when the time came.

Travis continued to move slowly as he backed out of his bathroom. He desperately wanted to use Calvin's name to let the man know he wasn't a threat. However, Travis still thought that would only make matters worse. So instead, he backed out of sight and left his bathroom door open.

Calvin would have to come out eventually if for no other reason than for Travis to take him back to The Witches Brew. It was with that thought still in mind, Travis entered his library and found a book to read while he waited for Calvin to finally make an appearance.

Chapter Eight

Cal remained in his cramped hiding place for almost forty-five minutes. His ears faced fully forward to listen intently for any sounds of movement in the house. He heard nothing after the first few minutes Travis had left the bathroom. It was almost as if the house was empty. However, he never heard a door open and close. Then again, Travis didn't seem to need conventional means to travel.

Finally, Cal's curiosity got the better of him now that his racing heart had calmed. Slowly, he belly crawled toward the open door and peeked out. He found a hallway which went in both directions. There were two open doors to his left and to his right the hallway seemed to open up into what Cal was sure was a living room he would be able to see if he was in his human form.

Moving in that direction was his best bet because he didn't want to become trapped in one of the two rooms at the other end of the hall. They were likely bedrooms. It was just as likely that Travis was asleep in one of them since the man worked the night before at the club. So, with that in mind, Cal hugged the wall along the hall and headed away from the bedrooms.

His assumption was correct when he reached the end of the hall. He paused to take in the room. The back of a soft looking leather couch faced him. It was bracketed by two dark wooden end tables on which there were beautiful stained-glass lamps. The lamps weren't turned on, but Cal couldn't help but wonder if the different colors of the glass would shine rainbow-like on the ceiling when they were. A chair matched the couch and could be seen on the other side of the end table in front of him. There was plenty of room for him to hide under the end table or behind the chair if he needed to, so he stepped on the plush gray carpet and moved slowly toward both.

Travis sat in his chair which was furthest from the hallway and with his feet up on his coffee table. He held the random book he grabbed from his library in his lap and his head was bent as if reading. He wasn't reading, though. No, he was stretching his senses out.

Calvin's scent grew stronger, so Travis knew the small garoul had left the bathroom and was approaching. He barely detected the soft pads of Calvin's paws on his hallway's hardwood floors before the sound disappeared altogether. Travis would have thought Calvin stopped in the hall if it weren't for his scent growing stronger. However, Travis knew that wasn't the case. Calvin had stepped onto his carpeted living room floor. He remained still and breathed shallowly even though he wanted to call out to Calvin and reassure him once more that he was safe.

Cal had been so focused on getting to a potential hiding place in the room that the sound of Travis' breathing didn't register in his ears until he reached the end table. Travis was in the room, but making no other noise aside from breathing. This encouraged Cal to peek around the end table in hopes of spotting the man. And, he did spot Travis. The sexy bartender sat in a chair reading. Cal really thought the man should have been asleep after a long night of work.

Travis caught Calvin's minute movement from over the top of his book without lifting his eyes away from the pages. Calvin was crouched low and all Travis could make out was his head and front paws. It was obvious Calvin was ready to flee if he felt the need to escape Travis.

Travis could no longer resist speaking. "I am a life drinker," Travis whispered. He was encouraged to continue when Calvin didn't bolt away. "I have a feeling you don't know what that is since I frightened you when we shadow stepped." Travis still didn't look up from his book. "There are a few of us that work at the club alongside of the garouls you probably sensed when you were there."

Cal tried not to panic at Travis' words, but he couldn't stop his heart from suddenly racing again. There was no way Travis should know he'd sensed the garouls in the club. The other garouls had never taken out the trash, so that could only mean Travis knew he'd been inside The Witch's Brew. Still, the question remained if Travis knew who he actually was and that they had already met. He felt it was a good bet that Travis did.

"The garouls at the club won't hurt you even though they are predators. Me and the other life drinker's won't, either." Travis paused. "I know you're scared since I can hear your heart racing, but you really have nothing to fear." Travis still didn't look up from his book. "I want to help you, but I can't do that unless you let me. I want to understand why you're scavenging around dumpsters and what has made you so afraid."

Travis finally looked up over the top of his book and even though Calvin had crept back further, he met the garouls pale green eyes before he spoke again.

"If someone has attacked you, hurt you, or even tried to kill you, we can help. There are those out there who try to kill anyone who isn't human. I don't know if you are aware of them, but they are what we call Hunters. Everyone at the club knows of them and we have dealt with them before. There is safety in numbers and we all want to help you, even if it isn't the Hunters that have you so afraid."

Cal's heart rate was continuing to race a mile a minute, but now for a totally different reason. Travis was aware of the Hunters. Not only Travis, but all of the supernaturals at The Witch's Brew. Not only aware of them, but had dealt with them before and just knowing this gave Cal hope that he just might survive his father.

Travis' words along with the newfound hope Cal might actually be able to have a life which didn't consist of him constantly living in fear gave Cal the courage he needed to stand. He slowly stepped forward and his eyes never left Travis' steel gray gaze while he cautiously crept closer to the supernatural. He kept his flank pressed against the soft leather of the couch and halfway to Travis, he leapt up onto the center cushion.

Travis was sure he hit the nail on the head for why Calvin was so afraid. He was heartbroken once more for the small garoul and the life Calvin must have led so far, especially if he was hiding, all alone, from Hunters. Still, that didn't stop the relief he felt wash over him when Calvin decided to come out from the safety of his end table. Travis took Calvin now sitting on his couch as a sign the man was beginning to trust him again. So, he closed his book and set it on his lap.

"You can shift, if you like," Travis dared to say and barely resisted using Calvin's name. "Or you can stay in that form if it makes you feel more comfortable." Travis waited for several more moments before he spoke again. "I'm going to make breakfast. Feel free to explore my home. Come into the kitchen to eat and if you decide not to shift I'll make you some chicken."

Cal watched Travis slowly lower his bare feet from the coffee table before he leaned forward and set his book down on the surface. Travis stood just as slowly and for once, Calvin didn't feel the urge to flee. It was clear Travis didn't want to startle him, especially when Travis walked around the chair he had been seated in instead of the space between the chair and the couch.

However, that didn't stop Cal from tracking Travis' movement as he walked into the kitchen. He had a clear view and Travis only looked back at him when he opened his refrigerator. Travis gave him a smile and a wink before he started pulling items out to make breakfast. It was the same smile and wink the sexy bartender shot at him in the club.

There was no reason for Travis to flirt with a cat and the fact that he was made Cal once again think Travis already knew who he was. *If that's the case, why hasn't he used my name?* Cal couldn't help but wonder.

He waited until Travis started cooking before he leapt down off the couch. He only spared a glance toward the kitchen to ensure Travis was still occupied with making breakfast before he trotted down the hall to investigate the other two rooms.

The room on the right almost took his breath away and Cal was sure he would've gasped in surprise had he been in his human form. Books. So many books. Cal had never seen so many books and he imagined this would be what a library would look like. He stepped into the room that had a lone chair and a table on which another stained-glass lamp rested.

Floor-to-ceiling shelves were packed with books and Cal was marveling at them so much that he almost knocked over a stack of books on the floor in front of him. Another glance around the room revealed more stacks of books. There was so many that Cal was sure they all couldn't be read in a lifetime. At least not a human lifetime, or even his although he had no idea how long he'd live.

His mother never shared a garouls expected lifetime. Maybe she thought they wouldn't ever reach it, so it wasn't important. However, he was sure one of the garouls at the club could tell him. It was that thought which made Calvin realize he'd already made up his mind to trust Travis and his friends to help him.

Since that was the case, there was no reason he shouldn't shift back into his human form. With a thought, he shifted and hesitantly stepped back into the hall. Cal stood there for a moment to reinforce his courage before slowly starting back down the hall to the living room.

Travis couldn't help but smile when he picked up the sound of footsteps in his hall under the sound of bacon sizzling away. He was immensely pleased and almost as relieved Calvin had shifted back into his human form. However, Travis didn't turn away from the stove to greet Calvin even though he knew the small garoul was coming into the kitchen. Hearing Calvin's soft footfalls on his carpet sounded loud compared to the silence his paws made earlier.

"Breakfast is almost finished," Travis informed. "Would you like some coffee, Calvin?"

Cal paused mid-step when Travis uttered his name. He shouldn't have been surprised at hearing Travis say his name since he had a feeling the man already knew who he was from the two times they'd met in the club. Still, it took him a moment to find his voice.

"Yes, please."

"Cups are above the coffee maker, sugar is next to it, and there is half-and-half in the fridge."

Travis still didn't look away from where he was removing the bacon from the pan and placing it on a paper towel.

"If you could make me a cup with two sugars and some cream, I'd appreciate it."

It was surreal standing in the kitchen discussing coffee with someone who wasn't Abe and knew what he was. The feeling more than likely had everything to do with Abe having been blind and Travis knowing exactly what he looked like in both forms. Regardless, Cal stepped toward the refrigerator and retrieved the half-and-half before he proceeded to make them both a cup of coffee.

"Breakfast is finished," Travis informed as he set the plate of bacon on the counter between two plated omelets. "Grab the silverware from the drawer in front of you, will you?"

Cal had no idea what to expect after he shifted and left the hall. It sure as hell wasn't this weirdly domestic encounter. Weird or not, he could admit it was relaxing to him. He got his first look at Travis since he shifted back to his human form when he turned around.

Cal was holding forks with his pinky and two mugs of coffee when he was greeted by Travis' friendly smile. Cal hesitantly returned the smile and set down the silverware and coffees without rounding the breakfast bar.

"Come eat before it gets cold," Travis invited and grabbed a slice of bacon at the same time he picked up his coffee and took a sip.

Cal slowly walked around the breakfast bar and took a seat next to Travis. They didn't speak while they ate and it wasn't until Travis stood to refill their coffees that Cal decided to break their silence.

"You knew it was me the entire time," Cal stated without any accusation in his tone.

Travis set down their coffees on the counter and began cleaning up their breakfast mess by picking up their plates.

"I did," he confirmed with a slight nod before he turned around to take the plates to the sink.

"How?" Cal was genuinely curious. "And since when?"

Travis had a feeling these would be the first questions Calvin asked once he'd earned the garoul's trust. So, he didn't hesitate to answer them.

"I'm sure you can sense other garouls and what they are. Maybe not exactly their type of animal since you seem sort of young." Travis held up his hand when it looked like Calvin was about to argue his age. All garouls were young to Travis since he'd been alive for longer than their life spans. "I only say that because I know you didn't recognize what I am. Most garouls are leery around my kind regardless of their size or how deadly their animal side is."

Travis paused to see what type of reaction Calvin would have to his declaration. Calvin just tilted his head slightly to the side as if he were attempting to hear something, so Travis continued.

"You can only sense whether another garoul is a predator or not, right?"

Cal nodded in agreement. "You still didn't answer my questions, though."

Travis finished putting everything in the dishwasher and turned back to face Calvin. He offered the beautiful man a smile. "Everyone has a unique scent to a life drinker."

"So, you can smell garouls regardless of whichever form we are in," Cal clarified.

"Not just garouls," Travis corrected. "Everyone. Humans, garouls, other life drinkers, and any other supernatural."

Cal had never heard of such a thing and his curiosity made him want to know more. "How is that possible?"

Travis continued to smile and only hoped his answer wouldn't scare, or worse, change Calvin's mind about letting Travis help him. But, he refused to lie to the man.

"I can smell their blood. Every living being smells different. It's an ability all life drinkers have, so we can differentiate who is safe to feed from and who is not."

Cal's eyes practically met his hairline. He wasn't expecting the sexy bartender who'd been so nice to him and seem so sincere with his offer to help to actually eat people. Cal stood from his chair and took a few steps back away from the breakfast bar. It didn't matter that Travis remained on the other side and hadn't made a single move to close the distance between them.

"You eat people?" Cal could hear the increase of pitch in his voice. "You brought me here to eat me?"

Calvin's reaction to him, to his kind, only confirmed what Travis thought about the garoul's age. It once more made him wonder why Calvin's family hadn't taught him about their world and the different types of supernaturals who remained hidden there.

"Calvin, you're safe with me and from my kind at The Witch's Brew. Life drinkers need the nutrition blood provides for us to survive, but we drink from bagged blood unless someone is willing to let us feed from them."

"How do I know you aren't lying?" Cal looked doubtfully at Travis.

"I haven't lied to you so far when I could've easily done so." Travis continued to level his friendly smile on Calvin while he leaned on his breakfast bar. "I'm going to stand up now and open my refrigerator to show you."

Cal took another step back and didn't take his gaze off Travis while the man stepped backward until he bumped into the counter next to the appliance. Slowly, as if Travis didn't want to freak him out more than the man already had, Travis opened one side of the refrigerator. Once the appliance was open, pulled out a drawer that seemed to have a false bottom and Cal could easily see the several bags of blood stacked in the drawer. Cal's freak out came down a notch.

"I would never feed off you or anyone else without permission," Travis assured with sincerity.

Cal believed Travis for some reason and his racing heart seemed one step closer to resuming its normal rhythm. Yet he still watched Travis intently when the man closed the refrigerator door and turned to refill his coffee.

Travis could hear Calvin's heartbeat returning closer to normal, so he slowly turned around to face him before speaking again. "I don't know where you have been sleeping, but I am sure you must be tired," Travis began. "My kind don't require sleep, so you can rest in my bed or shift and I can shadow step us back to the inside of The Witch's Brew."

"Why do you have a bed if you don't sleep?" Cal asked the first thought that popped into his head.

Travis chuckled and lifted a brow. "Sleep isn't the only thing a bed is good for."

Cal's cheeks heated. They heated even more when Travis shot him another one of those sexy winks.

"There is a lock on the bedroom door if you want to get some sleep," Travis added in the hope it would sway the younger man to stay.

He had a feeling if Calvin chose to return to The Witch's Brew he more than likely might not see the pretty blonde again after everything the garoul had just learned. That feeling only increased when Calvin spoke.

"Why would I have to shift for you to take me back to the club?"

"I can only take small things with me when I step between the shadows to travel because I am not old enough to take larger things like a person." Travis answered honestly. "I can call you an Uber if you would prefer, but I hope you will decide to stay."

Cal did want to stay even though he was unsettled by what he'd just learned about Travis' kind. However, like the last time he made a decision regarding the sexy bartender and The Witch's Brew, his pros and cons sheet flashed through his mind. The pros won out, once again.

"Okay, I'll stay," Calvin said with a small smile.

"I'll wake you when it's time to go if you're not up before then."

"Okay," Cal agreed and was only reassured more when Travis didn't move from leaning on his breakfast bar when he left the kitchen and headed toward the hall.

Chapter Nine

Cal closed and locked Travis' bedroom door before he turned and took in the room. Black and gray seem to be the theme. Plush black carpet covered the floor and the furniture was some sort of light gray wood which contrasted both. The headboard on the comfortable looking queen size bed matched the night tables and dressers.

A satin bedspread covered the bed and was black with random light gray geometric patterns. It matched the curtains which almost touched the floor as if there was a sliding glass door hidden behind them. Cal checked, and indeed there was. The doors led out to a small backyard and somehow Cal wasn't surprised to see grey pavers along with a black outdoor patio set. He was surprised to see a barbecue grill, even though he had breakfast with Travis before the man told him he needed to drink blood to survive.

Cal checked to be sure the doors were locked before he turned back to the perfectly made bed. The room was very masculine and seemed to fit Travis based on the little Cal had learned about the man. His mind was still reeling with all of the information when he lay atop the soft comforter. Travis' scent filled his nose the moment his head rested on the pillow. Cal wasn't expecting to smell the life drinker at all since Travis claimed he didn't sleep and only used his bed for other things. It made Cal wonder exactly how often those other things actually occurred.

Cal's swirling thoughts paused on that and seemed to get stuck on what it might be like if Travis did those other things with him. Cal wasn't a virgin, but he sure as hell didn't have a lot of experience with sex. He'd never had sex in a bed or even totally naked, either. There was no doubt Travis would be the more experienced of the two of them. Thoughts of how the sexy bartender's experience could be used on him were the last thing that filled his mind as he ignored his hard-on and drifted off to sleep.

Travis didn't even need to focus his sensitive hearing toward his bedroom in order to hear Calvin moving around on his plush carpet. He didn't hear the small garoul opening and closing his drawers or even checking his closet. Not that he had anything to hide if Calvin's curiosity got the better of him and he wanted to snoop. All cats were curious to an extent, especially the smaller breeds, so Travis was impressed at Calvin's restraint.

The sounds of his curtains being moved reached his ears and Travis wondered what Calvin thought of his small backyard. His yard was nothing special and typical of the others in his neighborhood. However, it was his favorite place to read after his library, especially in the nicer weather of the spring and fall. His yard was also one of the reasons he purchased the house instead of renting an apartment or buying a condo. George was the only other Brew family member who had a yard and they both enjoyed having everyone over for barbecues and the holidays.

The sounds from his bedroom finally quieted and all Travis heard was the steady settled beat of Calvin's heart and the small garoul's in and out breaths. Both indicated the beautiful man had fallen asleep. Travis smiled. Calvin falling asleep in his bed was a good sign the Calico trusted him to some extent, even if he did lock himself in the bedroom.

Travis enjoyed the sounds of someone sleeping in his bed as he continued to sit in his living room reading. It was a sound he could admit he missed hearing since he hadn't heard it in so long. In fact, he really couldn't remember the last time the peaceful sound filled his house. He really didn't bring his random hookups home and the rare times he did, he made sure they left after they both got what they both wanted.

It was just after two p.m. when Travis decided to text Mikael: *give me a call when you get a chance. Nothing is wrong. I just want to update you on the garoul.* Travis knew Mikael and Adam sometimes traveled the world during the day. Adam being so newly turned into a life drinker was why Mikael enjoyed showing him the world. It was because of this that Travis really didn't expect a reply right away. However, he got one when his cell phone began to vibrate.

"Has something changed since they began letting you pet him at night after work?" Mikael asked by way of greeting.

"Yes, *he* is actually sleeping in my bed as we speak," Travis stepped out onto his small front porch to speak to his boss and friend so the conversation wouldn't wake up Calvin.

"Did he just say the calico is sleeping in his bed?" Adam's voice was as clear as if Mikael had the phone on speaker. Travis knew that wasn't the case, though.

"Not because of that. Nothing happened between us," Travis was sure to clarify before he filled them in on everything which had transpired since he took out the club's trash the night before.

"Okay, we were right then. He's young... Did you ask him his age?" Mikael paused and waited for Travis to answer.

"No, but I plan to. Maybe not when he wakes up, but soon. He is still kind of skittish," Travis informed.

"His kind of garoul usually are, but I'm glad to hear his curiosity about you was enough to override his fear in order to trust you enough to go home with you." Mikael sounded pleased even though it was clear he was still concerned for the young garoul's safety.

"It seems we were right about the Hunters, as well," Mikael continued and Travis clearly heard Adam curse, "fuckers."

"He would be safer with us, so I'm going to continue to give him information on the community since it seems he knows next to nothing, in hopes it will build more trust between all of us," Travis informed them and only hoped his plan worked.

He hoped it worked more for Calvin's sake than for his own even though Travis was extremely attracted to the beautiful man. He was pretty sure Calvin was attracted to him, as well, but Travis wasn't sure if that attraction was misplaced because he was the first supernatural Calvin had any real interaction with since he'd been on the run. Regardless, no matter how much Travis wanted to act on his attraction, he wouldn't take advantage of Calvin in such a way.

"That seems like the best course of action," Mikael agreed. "Perhaps we can ask Cat or one of the others to educate him on garouls."

"Maybe, but...," Travis started and thought of Calvin's small size.

"But?" Mikael prompted.

"She is a predator, as is everyone else, so I'm not sure how that would go over with him. He's already skittish as hell, Mikael."

Travis understood that having one of his garoul family members teach Calvin about his kind was the best way to go since they would always know more about their community than the rest of the family. He just wasn't sure if Calvin could get over the fear Travis knew must be ingrained when it came to steering clear of predators.

"Well, maybe if we can get him to come into the club frequently enough and expose him slowly to the others, he'll realize he can trust them and they won't hurt him."

"Maybe," Travis agreed. "I'll see what I can do."

"Okay, we will see you tonight."

Mikael hung up and Travis leaned on his porch railing. He was enjoying the warm sunlight on his skin and the slight breeze when movement inside his house reached his ears. It was the sound of his bedroom door opening.

Travis decided he would remain where he was so he wouldn't startle Calvin by suddenly appearing in his living room after he was sure the garoul noticed it was empty. If Calvin was going to leave, he'd have to come out of the front door and Travis could talk with him again when he did.

A quick glance at the position of the sun told Travis it was barely four o'clock. Calvin had only slept for a few hours and Travis wasn't surprised at that considering his home would be unknown territory for the calico.

Cal startled out of his light sleep. He had no idea what had woken him. Still, it took him a few moments to remember where he was. It was the same every time he woke up in any of the crappy motel rooms he bounced around to and called home.

He wasn't in a shithole right now. No, the pale gray walls which almost looked white next to the black and multi-shades of gray geometric designs on the curtains reminded him exactly where he was: the sexy bartender's bedroom.

Cal lay in the comfortable bed for several minutes and strained to hear any movement from the other side of the closed and locked bedroom door. The lack of movement and the silence was almost unnerving.

However, he reminded himself that if Travis was still reading in the living room there wouldn't be any sound. Still, silent house or not Cal couldn't remain in the sexy bartender's bedroom forever, even if the bed he lay on was the most comfortable he'd ever experienced. Cal got up, unlocked the door, and stepped into the hall. The door across from him was open and he could easily see the comfortable-looking chair in the library was empty.

Travis must still be in the living room, Cal thought and was going to be relieved if his assumption was correct if it came to where the man was located.

That relief was short lived when he stopped in front of the bathroom door. The bathroom was at the end of the hall far enough that Cal had a clear view of the living room and the kitchen beyond. There was no sight of Travis. The bathroom door was still open and the light on, so Cal had no idea where Travis might be. The sun was shining through the curtains at the front of the house and provided too much light to cause any shadows. That alone told Cal that Travis didn't use shadows to travel somewhere like he had to bring Cal here.

Cal used the bathroom. He was still wondering where Travis could have gone when he stepped out into the hall. The attractive bartender had said he would wake Cal and take him back to the club. Cal didn't feel trapped here when Travis had told him that and he didn't feel trapped now. He had his cell phone so he could call an Uber to pick him up and take him back to his crappy motel room. All he had to do was verify Travis' address and make the call.

He continued to listen intently while he approached the front door. Cal still didn't hear anything before he opened the front door, so the last thing he expected to see was the muscular, white T-shirt covered back of Travis as he leaned against the porch railing.

To say Cal was surprised to see Travis enjoying the sun was an understatement. For some reason when Travis explained he was a life drinker and what that entailed, Cal immediately associated Travis' kind with

111

vampires. It only made sense he jumped to the conclusion Travis was a vampire because of the whole shadow travel thing, not sleeping, and especially the drinking blood to survive. Cal was seriously thrown for a loop at seeing Travis standing in direct sunlight and not frying to a crisp.

"You're outside," Cal spoke before he gave any thought to how his words could or would be perceived.

Travis hadn't turned around when he heard Calvin open his front door. He did so now. A smile spread his lips as he took in the beautiful man's sleep tousled hair. Travis wasn't offended by what he knew was Calvin's assumption that he was like a Hollywood vampire who died by sunlight. It was a misconception all norms had when they were exposed to his kind. Calvin's lack of knowledge where the supernatural community was concerned made the garoul almost a norm in that aspect. So no, he wasn't offended in the slightest.

Cal couldn't help but be reminded of how sexy Travis was when the bartender smiled. That smile was leveled on him once more and Cal couldn't help but return it.

"I am," Travis confirmed. "Life drinkers' aren't relegated to slinking around in the dark like Hollywood portrays vampires."

Travis' smile didn't leave his lips. Cal's did. He berated himself for offending the man with his ignorance even though Travis didn't appear offended at all. However, Cal still couldn't help but feel like shit about his assumption.

Cal looked away from Travis and seemed to study nothing in particular in his front yard. "Sorry, I didn't mean…"

Travis cut Calvin's apology off midsentence. "It's okay. You just don't know everything about my kind since I'm sure you've never met someone like me before."

"I haven't," Cal admitted with a small shake of his head and watched Travis from the corner of his eye as he leaned back against the porch railing. He tried to ignore how defined the muscles in Travis' forearms looked when the man stretched his arms out to the sides to rest his hands on the railing.

"Have you met many of your own?" Travis asked gently and didn't miss the fact that Calvin had yet to return his eyes back to meet his gaze.

Cal was quiet for several moments. Travis didn't press him for an answer and for that he was grateful since he wasn't sure he wanted to answer at all. The only other garoul he'd known was his mother and she really didn't teach him shit about their kind. Not even how to shift, but maybe that was something which didn't need to be taught.

No, all she taught him was how to stay alive by running and hiding amongst the norms. Oh, and how to sense other garouls and supernaturals. He wished she had taught him how to determine more than if they were just garouls or not norms. But, she hadn't and there wasn't fuck all he could do about his anger toward her since she was dead. That thought made him feel like hell because he shouldn't be angry at the one person who loved him enough to die for him. Shouldn't be, but somehow was, to the point his anger overrode his grief.

"I'm sorry. I shouldn't have asked," Travis whispered while he watched several emotions continue to make appearances on Calvin's beautiful face.

The sound of Travis' soft words snapped him out of the thoughts and memories of his mother. They also reminded Cal of what the sexy bartender had asked. The same sincerity he'd heard in Travis' tone when the man's concern for him made an appearance in the alley was present and what decided Cal's mind to answer honestly.

"That's okay." Cal forced himself to look back at Travis and met the man's pale gray eyes. For a moment, the brief thought that they matched the bedroom night tables flitter through his mind. It was a strange thought to have at the moment.

He gave Travis a small smile before he continued. "My mom was the only other garoul I've known."

The undertone of sadness and heartbreak was enough to make Travis believe Calvin's mother either left him to fend for himself, or worse, died before she could teach him what he needed to learn about the supernatural community.

"Would you like to meet others?" Travis asked carefully, hiding his hope.

Travis' innocent question made Cal stiffen. He was still leaning and totally relaxed against the porch railing. His tone was just as genuine. However, Cal's inner feline flooded him with the urge to run and hide. Not because of Travis. No, because he knew, just knew, the garouls the sexy bartender was offering to introduce him to were those that worked at The Witches Brew. Those were predators and could bat him around like a mouse, if not just kill him outright.

Fear at his words crossed Calvin's face and tensed the man's body. Travis regretted his offer immediately, but still felt he had to make it so Calvin understood he had an option not only to meet some of his kind, but also learn more about them and himself.

"You don't have to. Not unless you want or when you're ready," Travis told Calvin gently. "My family will still be there if you ever decide you want to meet them."

"They are predators," the thought was in the forefront of Cal's mind and escaped his lips.

"Yes." Travis wouldn't lie. "But, they'd never hurt you."

"You called them your family," Cal stated, but had no doubt Travis would hear the curiosity in his tone to know more, especially because he had no idea different supernaturals could have the same parents.

"They are." Travis smiled wider. "My chosen family. Some of them have been for a few hundred years, now."

Cal's eyes grew wide. He had no control over his eyebrows trying to become one with his hairline. His mother had never told him how long she'd been alive and for that matter, he never thought to ask since he assumed she was only twenty-seven when she had him. The way Travis talked made it sound like the garouls he worked with, the ones he called family, have been alive for much longer than he could ever imagine.

Does that mean I will live for hundreds of years? Was Cal's first thought before the next ambushed him, *how old is Travis then?* Cal didn't dare ask either question because he wasn't sure if he really wanted to know.

Calvin's wide-eyed reaction to his words had Travis mentally cursing himself again. It also reminded him of how little Calvin actually knew about the supernatural community. However, it was Calvin's reaction that not only confirmed the Calico garoul was young, but more than likely closer to the age he appeared than Travis first thought.

"Why don't I make us something to eat and I'll take you back to the club afterwards," Travis offered with the hope some food would calm the small garoul. He hated the shocked look his casual comment caused to appear on the pretty man's face.

"Um, no. Thank you." Cal looked away again. "I think I just want to go."

Travis made sure to keep the disappointment out of his tone when he spoke. "Alright. I can take you back to the club now if that's what you would like."

"I want to call an Uber," Cal said quickly and hoped the sudden panic he felt from learning he was talking to a being that was over a few hundred years old didn't leak into his tone.

Just the thought of how old Travis could be had his inner cat screaming to flee. Not because of anything Travis had done or said, but because he was sure there was just so much more he didn't know and suddenly no longer felt safe here.

The human side of him, not that he was actually human at all, told him rationally that Travis had been nothing but nice to him and sincere in his desire to help. However, the feline side of him only wanted to get far away to safety because of the unknown. Cal was pretty sure Travis wouldn't harm or hurt him, but his feline side won out.

Travis' long existence gave him the experience he needed to not show how he really felt. His expression, the kind concern he'd actually felt for the small Calico garoul never changed even though he was saddened by not only

Calvin's words, but his sudden and likely instinctive urge to flee. Travis could only hope Calvin's sudden feelings wouldn't prevent the Calico from returning to The Witches Brew.

"That's okay." Travis continued to offer Calvin a genuine and understanding smile. "Would you like me to call you one?"

Travis held up his cell phone which Cal hadn't even noticed was in his hand. He had his cell in the back pocket of his jeans and it was his paranoia which suddenly was riding him hard that made him pull it out. He didn't want Travis to know where he was staying even if he had every intention to change shitholes the moment he returned to the motel.

"The address here?"

Travis rattled off his house number and street name. He really wasn't surprised Calvin hadn't let him call an Uber to take the Calico back to wherever he was staying. Travis wasn't sure how long Calvin had been on the run since whatever happened with his mother happened. So, he assumed the pretty man didn't share where he stayed with anyone just so he could remain safe. The thought that this was the life Calvin had led for only God's knew how long in his short life broke Travis' heart once more.

"I'll wait with you, if that's okay," Travis said. "I'll just stand over here," he informed before he moved further away from the stairs that led from his porch to the walkway which ended at the curb.

Cal was only slightly relieved Travis had moved away from the porch stairs. He didn't really think Travis would prevent him from leaving since the man had been so nice and seemed to care about his well-being. But, then again he really didn't know the supernatural at all. It was with that thought Cal glanced down at his phone. The Uber app told him his driver was only two minutes away. Little waiting times for an Uber driver to pick him up was one of the perks he'd come to appreciate from living in a large city like Chicago. That and the ability to easily hide from his father which was the most important perk of all.

Calvin started down the stairs to walk to the curb, but forced himself to stop halfway there. He wasn't raised before his life went to hell to be impolite, so he turned back to face Travis where the sexy man who'd given him so much to think about stood.

He thought he saw an expression of concern or worry on the bartender's face, but if he had it was gone in a flash. Cal met Travis' light gray eyes and gave him a small smile even though his body still had the urge to run away and put as much distance between him and the man as possible.

"Thank you. For everything."

The sound of a car coming down the road, a car Cal was sure was his Uber ride, caused him to turn around and continue toward the curb.

"Will you come back to the club?" Travis' question reached his ears just as the Uber stopped at the curb

"I don't know," Cal replied without looking back at Travis. He opened the car door and was just stepping in when Travis spoke again.

"I hope you do," Travis barely paused before Cal's ass settled in the backseat of the car. "I like you Calvin, so I hope you do."

Those were the last words Cal heard as he was closing the car door. He had to force himself not to look back at Travis because even if he really wanted to, his feline side was still urging him to get away from the man as fast as he possibly could.

Chapter Ten

Cal changed motels twice before he finally worked up the nerve and returned to The Witch's Brew in his human form. The large garoul doorman gave him a nod even as Cal skirted past him into the club. Cal almost forgot how loud the club music was since he had not been inside in over a month. The lights on the dance floor were just as bright even though the lasers flickered through the smoky air to make colored designs. It was the same as the few times Cal had been here before, so he paid both little mind while he pushed through the crowd to get to what he was beginning to think of as his spot at Travis' bar.

It didn't take long for Travis to notice him and the man sent him a beautiful smile and a sexy wink. *Damn that man is gorgeous*, was Cal's first thought even though he'd seen Travis often while in his feline form. There was just something that made the supernatural even hotter seeing him in color as opposed to the muted grays and blues of his feline vision. Which, of course made sense.

Travis was more than happy to see Calvin standing at the end of his bar. He really hadn't expected the blonde to come back to the club after how skittish he'd been the last morning Travis had seen him at his home. He didn't hide his happiness at seeing Calvin while he pulled a cold bottle of water from the freezer and walked toward the man.

"I'm glad you decided to come back." Travis loved the shy smile Calvin gave him and Travis nodded toward the bottle of water he held. "Water or something else?"

"Water please," Cal replied.

He never consumed alcohol willingly. The few times he had were when he'd been injured and his mother gave it to him to help though his pain while she was patching him up. Alcohol did dull his senses and he needed to be on guard in case he crossed paths with his father. That was the same reason he'd never tried drugs.

"Sure." Travis passed the water over the bar and couldn't help but enjoy the sensation of Calvin's fingers brushing against his for a brief moment. "You don't drink? Not that there is anything wrong with that," Travis was quick to add.

"No." Cal opened the water and took a sip. "I don't like how it makes me feel."

Cal didn't like the memories which came along with the bitter taste of booze, either. He wasn't going to tell Travis about those, though.

Travis nodded. He really didn't know Calvin well, aside from when the beautiful man was in his calico form so he was having trouble reading how Calvin felt. As a bartender, Travis was excellent at reading people's emotions just from the expression on their face. Calvin's remained blank even though his eyes frequently darted around the club. His baby blue eyes were the only indication of his wariness at being in the club again. Other than that, Travis had no idea what he may have been feeling.

"Are you upset with me?" Travis asked and met Calvin's eyes when the garoul flashed them back at him. "For not telling you."

Calvin understood what Travis meant. He had analyzed his feelings over Travis knowing it was him in his calico form. He had come to the conclusion he wasn't angry at the bartender. Maybe he should be, but he wasn't. Travis had been too kind to him while he was shifted for him to be mad.

"No. I understand why you did it," Cal informed Travis and received a blinding smile for his reply.

"I'm glad because I meant what I said about wanting to get to know you better and helping you if you'd let me." Travis received another shy smile before Calvin took a sip of water. "Would you like to grab a bite after..."

Travis never had the chance to finish his question before Calvin tensed, took a step back away from the bar, and a look of fear filled his eyes. Travis turned halfway around to see what had frightened Calvin so badly.

Cat had been approaching the bar, tray in hand, and filled with empty glasses when she stopped mid-step. It was clear to Travis she had seen Calvin's reaction to her.

"It is okay, Calvin. Cat won't hurt you," Travis tried to assure the smaller feline when he turned back to the man. He almost felt like a broken record with how many times he'd already tried to reassure Calvin he was safe in The Witch's Brew. However, he would say it again and again if necessary until Calvin finally believed him.

Cal had dropped his bottle of water when he attempted to put as much space as he could between himself and the long blonde-haired garoul that was approaching him. The woman was smiling as she approached and even though her smile shifted to a more neutral expression when she stopped, Cal's inner feline still hissed and wanted to flee.

"She's a predator," Cal said softly, as if to himself, without taking his eyes off the woman.

It didn't matter that she was in her human form several feet away and not that of whatever she could shift into. Any sense of a garoul predator scared the ever-living shit out of Cal.

"Cat is a snow leopard," Travis told Calvin.

"Eeep!" The squeaky sound that escaped Cal's throat couldn't be helped.

He was backed into a corner and frozen to the spot. If Cal understood one thing about predators, especially feline ones like him, it was not to run. Cats big or small were ingrained to instantly pounce on anything that ran. They may not pounce with the desire to kill, but to play as well. Usually, before they *did* kill their toy. At least that was what Cal did every time he'd come across a mouse.

Knowing the waitress was a large cat only made Cal's fear worse. If she were anything other than a feline, Cal may have had a chance to escape. Or at least his death would be quick and not drawn out.

"Cat won't hurt you, Calvin," Travis repeated again in an effort to reassure Calvin.

He gave Cat a quick glance and she raised a questioning brow toward him. Travis tilted his head toward the opposite end of his bar and gave Cat a quick nod. She slowly backed away and Travis was grateful the club wasn't too crowded.

Cal watched the snow leopard garoul take a few steps back before she turned around and made her way to the other end of Travis' bar. Seeing the female predator turn her back to him calmed Cal's racing heart somewhat. Anytime a predator retreated was a sign that they were no longer interested in their intended prey.

"I... I think... I need to go," Cal stuttered out after he was sure the other garoul was far enough away that she couldn't catch him if he fled.

"I wish you would stay." Travis leaned on his folded arms that now rested on the bar.

Cal flicked his gaze back to Travis and met the man's kind eyes. He wanted to stay and knew his fear over the snow leopard garoul was likely worse than it should be since they were in a crowded club. His mother drilled it into him that their kind, and all supernaturals, would never let the norms become aware of their existence. It was this lesson and the club being full of norms which made Cal relax somewhat.

The more he flicked his gaze around the club, the more he realized the chances of a predator or any other garoul, for that matter, wouldn't risk revealing their world just to attack prey like him.

Travis could see that Calvin was starting to calm down and was encouraged the calico bobtail wasn't going to flee. "Let me take you out after I'm done for the night."

Cal hesitated for a moment before he replied, "okay."

"Great!" Travis smiled widely. "Let me get you a seat and another water."

Travis walked down the bar and pulled a cold bottle of water from the freezer. Adam was leaning against the end of the bar when Travis called out to him.

"Adam, can you grab a seat for my friend?"

"The small garoul?" Adam nodded to the blonde man standing between the wall and the bar in the far corner.

"Yeah, but maybe have Mikael take it over so you don't scare the hell out of him with your big ass." Travis chuckled at Adam's grunt.

Travis served three customers by the time Mikael stood at the bar next to a chair Adam retrieved from one of the standing tables.

"Let me warn him you are bringing the chair. He got a bad scare from Cat," Travis explained when Mikael raised a confused brow. "She's a predator."

"Ahh." Mikael nodded his understanding. "I'll wait till you are over there."

"Thanks."

Cal watched Travis talk to a big as fuck man wearing a bright neon yellow security shirt. The man's muscles look like his shirt would be a goner if he flexed. Cal really hoped that wasn't the man Travis was going to have bring him a chair. It didn't look like he was going to be that lucky when he saw the man grab a chair from a nearby table. However, the large man who could easily bench press him stopped with the chair near the bar.

Travis served a few customers which was likely why he didn't see the long blonde-haired man step up to the bar. The guy was super attractive, but not nearly as sexy as Travis. They spoke for a few seconds before Travis started heading back to him.

"Here you go." Travis set down the unopened bottle of water and received another shy smile from Cal when he opened it. "Mikael is going to bring a chair over for you."

Travis watched Calvin glance over his shoulder down the bar before his pale eyes which looked almost gray in the dim club's lights shot back to him. Travis gave him a sexy wink.

"He is like me, okay?" Travis dared to place his hand on top of Calvin's free hand which was resting on the bar. "He's nice. You'll see." Travis squeezed Calvin's hand. "I'll be right here."

Cal gave Travis a nod and barely turned his hand over so they were palm to palm. His gaze once more looked over Travis' shoulder and tracked the blonde carrying a chair toward them. Cal didn't take his eyes off the man when he stopped next to him, either. Thankfully, the guy stopped a few feet away with the chair separating them.

"Hi. I am Mikael. You must be Calvin." Mikael smiled politely and held out his hand.

Cal glanced at Travis and the sexy bartender gave his hand a small squeeze before letting go. Cal could tell the blonde man, Mikael, was a supernatural, but not a garoul. If Travis hadn't told him Mikael wasn't the same type of supernatural as he, Cal would've had no clue what he was at all. It was this thought which made him concentrate on the vibe he felt from both men. It was distinct and Cal memorized it so he'd be able to recognize another life drinker if he ever met one.

Cal relaxed even more and held out his hand to shake. "Nice to meet you."

"You, too. Let me put this chair where you're standing." Mikael continued to offer a soft smile.

Cal stepped away from the bar far enough for Mikael to place the chair where he'd been standing. He waited for the man to return to his original spot at the bar before he took his seat.

"Thank you."

"Sure thing." Mikael leaned on the bar and glanced at Travis.

"Do you want a drink?" Travis asked Mikael.

"Just a water," Mikael replied.

Cal was still watching Mikael when Travis walked away. He was still focused on the vibe he was picking up from the man. That and reminding himself he had no reason to think this supernatural would hurt him. Mikael wasn't a garoul and they were in the middle of a club, as well.

"Mind if I hang out with you for a bit?" Mikael asked without looking away from where Travis was fixing drinks.

"I… I guess," Cal forced himself the reply.

He could admit he was curious about the supernatural. Aside from his mother and now Travis, he never had the chance to get to know someone else from the supernatural community. Being attacked by supernaturals that joined the Hunters didn't count as far as he was concerned.

Mikael nodded, but didn't close the foot or so space between them. Both of them had no difficulty hearing one another even though the club music was thumping around them. Mikael didn't say anything else before Travis returned and blindly set down Mikael's water in front of him. His sole focus was on Calvin and when the pretty garoul shot Travis a glance, Travis smiled in return.

"You'll be fine with Mikael. He won't let anything happen to you while I finish up working for the night."

Cal caught himself smiling at Travis. He wasn't sure when it happened, especially since he fled the man's house, but he realized he actually trusted Travis. If Travis said he was safe with Mikael, then Cal believed him even if he was still struggling to believe the garoul predators in the club wouldn't harm him.

"Alright." Cal took a sip of water and shifted in the chair so that his back was against the wall and he was facing Mikael.

Travis was relieved to see the change in Calvin's body language. The calico bobtail was still wary, but nowhere near as skittish or paralyzed with fear like he had been when he spotted Cat. Travis gave Calvin's hand another squeeze before he turned around and went back to work.

"I've known Travis for a long time," Mikael said casually. "He's a good guy. Sometimes he cares too much, but he can't be faulted for caring."

Cal already knew this about Travis, so he didn't bother commenting on Travis' compassion and desire to help him. However, Mikael mentioning knowing Travis for a long time sparked his feline curiosity.

"How long?"

Mikael finally turned to look at Calvin. "A few hundred years, now."

Cal's eyes grew wide like they had when Travis had mentioned his age before, and he purposely looked Mikael over from head to toe. He then shifted his gaze to Travis' fit body moving behind the bar. Cal may be only twenty-four, but he felt confident in his assessment that neither man looked older than their early thirties. He finally returned his attention back to Mikael and was greeted with a grin.

"Travis said you didn't know much about our kind and don't know much about the community," Mikael stated neutrally because he wasn't criticizing the young garoul.

Everything Mikael said was true. Cal couldn't deny it and once more anger spiked toward his mother for leaving him so unprepared in the event of her death. Now, she *was* dead and Cal was floundering in a sea of the unknown when it came to the supernatural community he was born into.

"I still don't," Cal replied in answer to both of Mikal's observations.

Mikal nodded. "That is understandable when one is on the run from Hunters at such a young age. You are young, aren't you Calvin?"

Cal really wasn't surprised at Mikael's mention of Hunters because he had mentioned it to Travis. He was surprised that Travis hadn't instinctively known how old he was or even asked his age aside from knowing he was young.

Perhaps someone a few hundred years old could already tell how young I am.

"Compared to you two, I am young." Cal smiled shyly. "I guess by norms standards, I am as well. I'm only twenty-four."

Mikael nodded again. "I won't ask you for any more personal information." Mikael smiled. "But, you should know that you can tell Travis anything. He only shared your history of Hunters because it may affect my family and I will do *anything*, anything, to protect my family."

Cal noticed Mikael's friendly expression turn scary serious when he mentioned his family. It shot a bolt of fear through him and he leaned back to put a few more inches between them. He didn't feel the same level of fear that had paralyzed him when the snow leopard approached, but the type of fear which told him Mikael could be an extremely violent man if the situation called for it. Mikael's expression returned to the friendly one that graced his lips and the sudden and quick change made Cal physically shudder.

"You and Travis are brothers?" Cal managed to ask without stuttering and Mikael's chuckle caught him by surprise.

"No. We are just longtime friends."

"But you mentioned family," Cal prompted because he was suddenly confused by the life drinker's proclamation.

"All my employees are my family. It's my responsibility to keep them safe, and I do. Regardless of whom they are in the community. The ones here are my family and I won't allow anything to happen to them."

Cal had no doubt Mikael could see the wheels spinning in his mind. "You own the club?" Cal could hear the surprise in his tone.

"I do," Mikael confirmed. "So, you have my word you *are* safe here whenever you come in."

Cal's gaze flicked over Mikael's shoulder and he pressed back into the wall again. A brown-haired man in a neon yellow security T-shirt was clearly approaching them. The guy was closer than the snow leopard waitress had been, so Cal knew he wasn't a garoul. Knowing that prompted Cal to focus on the vibe he was feeling from the guy. Cal was sure the guy was another life drinker by the time he smiled at them.

"Richard," Mikal greeted without breaking his gaze from Cal. "You really need to use your earpiece." Mikael grinned and winked at Cal before he turned to look at the security guy.

"It's impersonal and annoying," the guy, Richard, complained.

"Did you need something?" Mikael didn't seem perturbed by the interruption.

"Yeah. Rita suspects a problem between a few new visitors to the club."

"Really?"

Cal thought Mikael stern expression didn't match the almost gleeful sound of his question. It sent a chill down his spine and distracted him from the thought there was a problem in the club which likely had something to do with supernaturals.

Mikael turned back to him. "It was a pleasure talking to you, Calvin. I hope to get to know you better in the future."

Cal didn't even have the opportunity to reply before the club owner walked away from where he'd been leaning against the bar. Cal watched as the crowd seemed to part before Mikal and the security guy followed in his wake. It wasn't until the club goers seemed to flood back into the space behind Mikael and Richard that Cal turned his attention back down the bar toward Travis.

Travis had just set down a drink for a customer, but his eyes weren't on the money being handed to him. No, they were on Cal and when Travis shot him another wink and a smile before he turned toward the register, Cal was flooded with warmth. He was sure it was that warmth which had him returning the sexy bartender's smile.

Travis had been keeping an eye on Calvin while the cutie talked with Mikael. Not because he didn't trust his friend and boss, because he did. No, he watched for any telltale sign Calvin's fear was making another appearance. Mikael *could* be scary, but that side of the man usually only made an appearance when his protectiveness for the family came out.

He was relieved to see Calvin seemed relaxed for the most part. Aside from whatever Mikal had said to cause a temporary look of surprise to cross Calvin's beautiful face. He would ask Mikal what that was all about later.

Travis didn't hear anything in his earpiece, but he wasn't too surprised to see Richard approach Mikael for whatever issue he needed addressed. The life drinker never used his earpiece even after working at the Brew for more than six months. It was frustrating for them all, but it just was what it was. He watched Mikael and Richard leave the bar before he headed down to Calvin.

"Here you go." Travis gave Calvin another bottle of water even though the man hadn't finished his first one yet.

"Thanks." Cal smiled at Travis and he didn't feel shy about it, for once.

"That's beautiful." Travis regretted his words the moment he spoke them because Calvin's smile disappeared and a look of confusion crossed his face.

"What is?" Cal had no idea what Travis was talking about. He even glanced behind him to determine what Travis could have seen to warrant such a comment.

"Your smile," Travis admitted honestly and would've sworn Calvin blushed.

"Your friend, I mean boss, seemed nice," Cal said to shift the focus off him.

"He's both, but more my friend than boss. All of us who work here would say the same." Travis grinned. "But you're right, he is nice." Calvin nodded in agreement. "I'll be done soon, so don't go anywhere."

"I won't," Cal replied and meant it as he settled down to watch Travis finish his shift.

Chapter Eleven

Cal continued to watch Travis work until the club lights came on and the patrons shuffled toward the front door. The entire time he was aware of the other predator garouls in the club, but none of them approached him. For that, he was grateful and was pretty sure their distance was due to Travis' intervention.

Only two of The Witch's Brew employees came close to the short end of the bar. Cal focused on them. One was a short norm female and the other was the huge ass guy who held the chair earlier. Cal recognized the vibe the guy gave off. He was a life drinker like Travis, Mikael, and the other security guy.

The bar emptied and only employees were left. Cal could sense two of the women were garouls, predator garouls, aside from the snow leopard waitress. The vibe he received from the large doorman was still confusing. He felt like a predator, but not really. Cal *was* sure he was a garoul. There was another woman who was strikingly beautiful and Cal was more than sure she wasn't a norm, even if he had no idea what she was. She gave him a bright smile and Cal knew it wasn't only her smile that made him feel less threatened.

Still, Cal remained where he was seated and watched The Witch's Brew employees go through their closing routine. Well, he actually watched Travis more than anyone else. Before long it was only he and Travis left in the club. It didn't escape Cal's notice at the time nor the fact that for the last two weeks he'd already been shifted and waiting for Travis outside.

"I'm just taking these out, then we can go," Travis leveled another blinding smile on him.

"I'll help," Cal offered since he knew it usually took Travis two or three trips to take out the club's nightly trash.

"You don't have to."

Cal was already walking down the long side of Travis' bar. "I don't mind."

Cal really didn't, either. At some point during the night he realized he was looking forward to going out with Travis after the club closed. Travis *did* make him feel safe. It was a strange feeling since he hadn't felt it since before his first time shifting at puberty. It was also a feeling that seemed to lift a weight off him to make him feel lighter.

His mother would kill him for feeling this way if she weren't dead already. She was probably turning over in the ditch that was her grave. Cal pushed away the thoughts of his mother and everything she taught him about staying alive. He especially didn't allow thoughts of all the things she never taught him which he should know to fill his head. No, all he wanted to focus on was how, or maybe what, Travis was making him feel.

Travis could almost feel the change in Calvin as the stunning blonde approached. He looked more relaxed than Travis had ever seen him before and Travis couldn't believe how suddenly he was turned on. Travis didn't hesitate to pick up two bags of trash and hold one in front of him to hide his painful erection. He gave Calvin another smile when the man picked up two bags of trash and stood next to him. It only took them a few minutes to throw away all of it.

"Let me call us a ride," Travis offered when they started walking toward the front of the club and he did. "Less than five minutes," Travis informed as he stood shoulder to shoulder with Calvin.

"Are we going far?" Cal asked and tried not to think about how much he was enjoying the body heat he could feel rolling off Travis.

"No. The diner isn't too far."

They settled into a comfortable silence while they waited for the Uber to arrive. Travis didn't want to start a conversation with Calvin that they would have to pause once they got in the car. He was sure Calvin felt the same way. Their Uber arrived and less than ten minutes later they were dropped off in front of the all-night diner.

There wasn't a hostess to seat them, so they seated themselves in a booth furthest from the door and cash register. Cal would've rather sat near the kitchen door so he would have an alternative escape route if his father walked into the diner. But, he trusted Travis to help him escape if that happened. Still, though, he couldn't break his habit of sitting where he could face the door regardless of how much he trusted Travis.

The waitress had given them a few minutes to look over the menu before she came over to take their order. They both ordered, eggs, bacon, and toast for Travis and French toast and sausage links for Calvin. They both ordered coffee, as well, and didn't speak until the waitress set down their cups and returned to the counter by the register.

Travis had been watching Calvin since they sat down. It didn't escape his notice the small garoul took a seat facing the door or the nervous glances in that direction which he tried to hide. Calvin was no longer as relaxed as when they left The Witch's Brew. Travis was sure it had something to do with Calvin realizing Betty wasn't a norm.

He wasn't exactly as skittish as Travis knew he could be, but Calvin did look like he would bolt if something bad startled him enough. It dawned on Travis that Calvin wasn't likely used to being so exposed in a public place. He should've considered Calvin would be unnerved if he had been on the run and hiding from Hunters for some time.

"We're okay here." Travis held out his hand across the table. He hoped Calvin would take it and breathed a mental sigh of relief when he felt Calvin's warm palm rest atop his.

"Betty is a dream walker and Don, the cook, is a changer."

"A what and what?" Cal couldn't help but ask.

He had no idea what type of supernatural a dream walker and changer were or what they could do even if Betty's ability seemed like a given.

Betty delivered their order and smiled at them. "Enjoy."

Travis waited until Betty returned to her spot by the register before he explained. "A dream walker is just that. They can astral project and visit the dreams of those they've met."

Cal's glance shot toward Betty. He wasn't comfortable with meeting someone who could spy on his dreams whenever they felt like it. There were far too many nights he relived the horror of his father chasing him and his mother or what his imagination conjured his father would do to him if he was ever caught. Then, of course, there were his most recent erotic dreams about Travis. As sporadic, but more frequent as they were becoming, he sure as hell didn't want anyone spying on those.

Travis squeezed Calvin's hand. He was surprised the man hadn't moved his from Travis'. "Betty won't randomly visit you just because you've met. She mostly locates missing people and visits her family."

"Oh, well, that's good." Cal did feel a sense of relief knowing that about the dream walker. "And a... Changer... Is what?"

"They are someone who can change their appearance, but you don't have anything to worry about when it comes to Don," Travis answered and ate a piece of bacon.

"That's kind of scary," Cal admitted and poured syrup over his French toast.

"They can be when they've joined the Hunters," Travis informed.

He immediately regretted his words when Calvin stiffened and his gaze bounced between the kitchen window and the diner door. Travis felt Calvin's palm twitch under his, but the small garoul still didn't pull away.

"Hey." Travis squeezed Calvin's hand again.

"I felt she wasn't a normal when we walked in." Cal caught himself looking at the waitress again before he shifted his gaze back to Travis. "I knew she wasn't a garoul or like you, but I figured you wouldn't bring me somewhere I wouldn't be safe."

Travis' smile returned. "You figured correctly." Calvin must've heard the 'but' coming in Travis' tone because the beautiful blonde arched a questioning brow.

"But?" Cal asked because he just *knew* there was a 'but.'

"You're adorable." The words slipped off Travis' tongue without thought. Calvin's eyes grew wide and Travis cleared his throat before he continued. "But." Travis grinned. "Aside from wanting to take you on a date, I thought it would be good for you to be able to recognize a dream walker and a changer."

"A… Date?" Cal shuttered. He was well aware his focus should've been on the rest of what Travis said, but he couldn't get past that this *was* a *date*.

He'd never been on a date before, but he understood the concept. One person asked another to do something so they could get to know one another and or just enjoy each other's company. Most dates, at least from what he'd learned from watching TV, led to sex. That thought had him going from soft to hard in record time and so fast he almost groaned in pain.

"Yes," Travis answered before it dawned on him that Calvin may have never been on a date before or even in a relationship for that matter. Hell, if that was the case then the small garoul was likely a virgin, as well. Calvin being a virgin didn't change anything about how Travis would court the young man.

"Don't be offended," Travis started. "But have you been on dates before?"

Cal felt his cheeks heat up and he had to look away from Travis. He took a moment to hide behind his coffee mug by taking a drink.

"I wouldn't call them dates," Cal finally managed to reply.

Travis had to stop himself from raising a surprised brow at Calvin. It seemed Calvin may not be as virginal as Travis first thought. However, Travis pushed the thoughts away of how little or much experience Cal had with men and shifted in his seat. He'd been hard since Calvin blushed and smelling the man's arousal didn't help his poor dick go down any, either.

Travis had to clear his throat again. "I'd like to introduce you properly to Betty and Don. Being around them for a bit should let you get a vibe for what they are and help you recognize others of their kind when you come across them."

Cal wasn't ready to stand only a few moments before, but now the Travis mentioned the two other supernaturals in the diner he felt his arousal dampen. Which he wasn't sure if he was relieved or disappointed about. All of his sexual encounters either consisted of his hands or nameless, faceless quick release in darkened alleys. He'd never cared to see the faces of the few men he'd been with and Cal was okay with that. More than okay.

However, now he could definitely not only see, but appreciate Travis' looks. Still, Cal understood his attraction toward Travis had way more to do with just how unbelievably sexy the bartender was. Granted, Travis had a body to die for, but it was Travis' kind and caring nature which had Cal totally hooked on the man. It was those thoughts that made Cal realize he was definitely more disappointed than relieved by Travis mentioning the other non-norms in the diner.

"Calvin?"

Travis easily saw the small garoul was lost in thought. He didn't appear afraid or tense like he had when they came into the diner, so Travis couldn't help wondering what he'd said to cause the gorgeous blonde to get so lost in thought.

"Cal," Cal replied almost absently as he tried to get his mind back on track.

Travis chuckled. "Okay, Cal. Want to meet Betty and Don?"

"Umm... Yeah, I guess. I mean I need to learn about others in our community, right?" Cal was sure he sounded like he was trying to convince himself more than just agreeing with Travis. He was also sure Travis noticed, as well.

"Alright." Travis stood and took Cal's hand in his properly before tugging the younger man to his feet.

Travis fully expected Cal to let go of his hand once Cal stood next to him. He was more than pleased that wasn't the case. Travis would enjoy every second he could get touching Cal, even if Cal only held his hand for reassurance or to bolster his courage.

"Hey, Betty," Travis called out as they approached the waitress.

"I would've brought your check to you, Travis." Betty smiled wide. "But I can see where you might be impatient to get your boyfriend home." Betty chuckled and shot Cal a wink.

Cal could feel his cheeks heating again. He never had a boyfriend before and wasn't sure if one date with Travis meant they were boyfriends or not.

"Can you ask Don to come out from the back?" Travis asked once they stopped near the stools closest to the cash register.

"Now, I know there couldn't be a problem with the food." Betty continued to smile and handed Travis their check.

"The food was delicious, as always," Travis reassured Betty.

"Okay," she replied and Cal could easily see that Travis' request for the cook to come out had sparked her curiosity.

"How's it going, Travis?"

Cal took in the man who came through the swinging door that led into the kitchen. He wasn't sure what he was expecting, but the portly, almost balding man was not it. Since changers could change their appearance, according to Travis and hence their name, Cal couldn't figure out why this man who looked to be in his fifties chose to look this way. If it weren't for the specific supernatural vibe Cal felt in the man's presence, he would've never known the man wasn't a norm based on his unassuming appearance.

"I'm doing good, Don." Travis shook Don's outstretched hand. "I wanted you to both meet Calvin. Cal."

"Pleasure to meet you, sweetie." Betty continued to smile at them.

"Good to meet you, Cal," Don greeted and stretched his hand out to shake.

"You, too." Cal shook Don's hand, but was concentrating on how different Betty and Don felt from garouls and Travis' kind.

"Cal hasn't met anyone like you guys, so I thought he should," Travis informed the supernaturals who worked in the diner.

"Really?" Don asked at the same time Betty spoke, "oh, you poor thing. You must be young indeed."

Cal nodded because he really wasn't sure what to say since he had no idea how long his kind lived. He was relieved when Travis replied for him.

"Cal lost his family to an accident and is new to the area."

"Oh, honey," Betty said with sympathy and for a moment Cal thought the dream walker was going to hug him. He was glad she restrained herself.

"Sorry to hear that," Don said sincerely. "I lost my family a long time ago, but they are always with me. They live on in my heart and memories."

The small smile Don offered him told Cal the man believed his words. Cal was happy the man found solace in his memories of his family. He only wished he could do the same where his mother was concerned. Hell, he couldn't even feel that way about the memories he had before puberty. His shift and everything that had happened since ruined *every* good memory he'd ever had where his parents were concerned. So once again, Cal just nodded.

Travis spent a few minutes catching up with Betty and Don to give Cal time to get used to how they felt. Only exposure to other supernaturals would allow Cal to recognize them and their imprint to settle in his mind. The more often he could expose Cal to the various supernaturals in their community, the faster Cal would be able to identify what species they were from just being in their proximity.

Travis had every intention to bring Cal back to the diner for another date if the small garoul would go out with him again. He was pretty sure Cal would, but Travis wasn't above using the excuse Cal should get more exposure to Betty and Don to easily recognize their kind faster.

"Well, we're going to head out," Travis said to Don and Betty by way of goodbye. "I'm sure we will see you again soon."

"Sounds good," Don agreed. "And remember Cal, you can come in any time. You don't have to be with this one, either." Don grinned and gave Cal a wink.

Cal couldn't help but smile. He was still smiling when Travis opened the diner door and Betty called out to them.

"You boys look good together. You treat that boy right, Travis."

"I plan to, Betty, I plan to," Travis replied with a glance back over his shoulder.

Cal felt his cheeks warm again not only from Betty's words, but from Travis' reply. It wasn't until they were out the door and Cal felt the cool air on the palm of his hand that he realized he'd held Travis' hand the entire time they'd been in the diner. He missed Travis' touch, but was hesitant to reach out and take the man's hand again.

Travis called for an Uber and started to put his phone in his back pocket when he realized he didn't have any way to contact Cal. That was something he had to fix because waiting for Cal to just show up at the Brew, just wouldn't do.

"Can I get your number?" Travis turned to Cal.

There was only an inch or so difference in their height. Travis had to restrain himself from tilting Cal's chin up that tiny bit so he could kiss him.

Cal had to take a moment to remember his number since he only used his phone to order take out online or to request an Uber. Having a cell phone was a new thing for Cal. He never had one before he hit puberty and shifted for the first time. He never had one while on the run with his mother, either, because they were inseparable.

It wasn't until he lived with Abe for over a year, that he bought one. Or rather, Abe bought him one. Cal had argued with the old blind man who taken him in, but the moment Abe told him he'd feel better if Cal had one 'just in case,' Cal caved.

"Yes," Cal rattled off his cell phone number.

Travis didn't hesitate to create a contact for Cal and send him a message. The way Cal startled when his back pocket dinged made Travis think Cal had never received a text message before. Maybe he hadn't.

"That's my number." Travis smiled and watched Cal intently as he retrieved his cell phone from his back pocket. "You can call me anytime. If I'm at work it might take me a bit to get back to you, but since I don't sleep…" Travis shrugged as if that said it all.

"Okay." Cal gave Travis a smile.

He was both nervous and excited over the thought of texting or calling Travis whenever he wanted to speak to the sexy man. Cal had no idea what he would say, but they hadn't had a problem talking with one another so far. He was sure he would think of something.

"Ah, here's your ride." Travis nodded toward the Honda Civic that pulled into a parking spot in front of the diner.

"My ride?" Cal asked before he thought better of it.

146

"Well, I'm happy to ride with you to wherever you are staying, but I didn't want to assume that was what you wanted, yet."

Cal was blown away by Travis' consideration for his privacy in regards to where he was staying. It would be easy for him to change motels after he was dropped off if he didn't want Travis to know where he was staying. He thought of doing just that so he could spend a little more time with Travis. It would only be for the length of a ride, though, because then Travis would head home. Still, if Travis rode with him he would need to call another Uber to take him home if he didn't stay with Cal for a bit longer. Or, the Uber could just drop Travis off first since Cal already knew where the hot bartender lived.

"You could get dropped off first," Cal suggested hesitantly.

"It will be faster if I go on my own." Travis continued to smile at Cal.

"Oh, yeah, okay." Cal had totally forgotten about the shadow travel thing Travis could do.

"And safer for you." Travis stepped closer to Cal. They were almost chest to chest and Travis' hands itched to touch. All thoughts of not taking advantage of Cal seemed to have fled Travis' mind. "If we rode together, I don't know if I'd be able to keep my hands to myself."

Once more Cal felt his cheeks heat. "Um... Okay."

Cal's blush and shy smile didn't do a damn thing to mute Travis' suddenly runaway libido. "May I kiss you good night?"

Travis wasn't sure what Cal's reply or reaction would be to his request, but the sudden scent of arousal that wafted off Cal gave him hope the smaller garoul would say yes.

Cal didn't answer Travis with words. Instead, he hooked his fingers in the belt loops of Travis' jeans and closed the few inches between them. A sigh escaped his lips when he felt Travis' hands come up to cup his face. Travis held his face and just looked at him for what felt like forever before he leaned in and pressed his lips against Cal's gently.

"Good night, beautiful," Travis whispered against Cal's lips before dropping his hands.

"Good night, Travis."

Cal watched Travis until the Uber drove him out of sight of the man.

Chapter Twelve

Cal would swear he still felt the press, the heat, and the tingling sensations from Travis' kiss when he closed the door to his crappy motel room. Just thinking of the kiss made his knees feel weak. He leaned on the door because he wasn't sure he could make it to the bed, yet.

It was his first kiss and enough TV and movies told him Travis' kiss was chaste. There was no craziness of mouths trying to devour each other. No, Travis' lips barely touched his. He hadn't expected Travis to slobber all over him like kisses on TV seem to imply. In fact, he wasn't sure what to expect.

However, what he didn't expect was for such a gentle touch to make his knees still feel weak or his lips to still tingle for so long after their kiss. Granted, it had only been ten minutes or so since Travis' mouth pressed against his. But, Cal swore he could still feel the tingles. He raised a hand to his lips and wished the caress of his fingers tracing them was Travis' mouth.

Cal wasn't sure how long he leaned against his motel room door and relived Travis' kiss. Light was coming in around the edges of the curtains, but it wasn't the glare of the sun that indicated it was midmorning which finally had Cal moving toward the bed.

No, it was the increasing pressure in his jeans. His cock was so fucking hard, ached so bad, it was almost painful to take the few steps from the door to the bed. He didn't even make it all the way before he had his jeans unbuttoned and unzipped. The relief from just undoing his jeans was immense, but only because the confining pressure of his jeans was gone.

Cal wasn't sure when he consciously lay on the bed, pushed his jeans and briefs down, or grabbed the lube that sat on the chipped and scratched up night table. No, the first thing he became fully conscious of was the feel of his hand wrapping tightly around his slicked-up dick.

The moan that escaped his throat was loud, but he gave no thought to the sound escaping his lips or who might hear him through the thin walls. His mind was bombarded with how good it felt to be touched. It didn't matter if it was his own hand. Relief was what he sought. It was what he needed.

He replayed Travis cupping his face and gazing in to his eyes as if he were the most precious thing in the world. No one had ever looked at him that way before. Cal could practically feel the heat of Travis' palms on his cheeks and the man's thumbs gently caressing his jaw as if Travis lay atop him doing it again. In his mind, Cal felt Travis' weight pressing him down into the mattress while he bucked up against him.

Cal moaned loudly again in the silence of the room. He wanted this feeling to last forever, but the moment he envisioned Travis leaning down and pressing their lips together, Cal exploded. His fist stilled even if his thrusting hips didn't and he arched up off the bed with a shout.

Cal came back to himself at some point. His hand rested on his still semi hard cock and he was a self-caused debouched mess. Cum not only coated his fist, but covered his stomach. Well, what little of his stomach was exposed since his T-shirt seemed to take the brunt of his release if how wet and stuck to his skin it was any indication. His jeans were barely pushed down his thighs. In fact, Cal could still feel them covering his ass.

Cal sat up and swung his legs over the side of the bed. It was then he realized he hadn't even kicked off his sneakers before he laid down in his blind urge to achieve relief. He couldn't help but chuckle.

"Hell, if this is what remembering Travis' kiss does to me," Cal said aloud to his empty room and shook his head without finishing his thought before he walked to the bathroom, dropping clothes in his wake, to shower.

Travis watched the Uber car which took Cal to wherever he stayed drive away. Once it was out of sight he walked back into the diner. The sun was coming up and he needed the shadow the closed restroom door could provide.

"See your boyfriend off?" Betty grinned.

"Not my boyfriend, but working on it," Travis replied as he headed toward the restroom.

"It'd be good to see you settle down," Betty started. "You've been doing the hit-and-run thing for too long."

Travis glanced over his shoulder. He had only been in Chicago for five years since Mikael moved their family here, so there was no way Betty could know how long he'd been alone. At least not as actual fact, but for all he knew, she could sense how long it had been since he'd been in a relationship. Now however, was not the time to encourage this line of conversation. Nope. Now was the time to take his ass home.

"I'm working on it, Betty," Travis repeated and stepped into the men's room.

He ignored the grunt from Betty which was her reply and flicked off the light to plunge the small space into darkness. Travis shadow stepped and from one second to the next he traveled between the diner restroom and his bathroom. Travis started stripping and was halfway naked before he flicked the switch to cause the bathroom lights to flood the space. He turned on his shower and finished undressing. By the time the water was a comfortable temperature and he stepped beneath the massaging spray, his mind had already replayed his date with Calvin, Cal he corrected, two times.

It wasn't until they were almost halfway through their breakfast that Cal finally returned to his relaxed state Travis witnessed by the time they had left the Brew. It made him feel good Cal trusted him enough to relax, but Cal's lack of fear or skittishness wasn't what Travis' mind focused on. No, it was the fact that Cal had let him hold his hand for almost the entire time they'd been on their date. He'd also let Travis kiss him goodnight.

If nothing else, it showed how much Cal trusted him. He could admit he was extremely surprised and not sure what had changed for Cal considering the way the small garoul fled from his house the last time he was here. Not that Travis was complaining because he sure as hell wasn't.

He wanted to know Cal better and actually cared for the pretty blonde more than he should. Well, likely more than someone who just wanted to help another supernatural who obviously needed help. Travis considered himself to be very self-aware of his feelings, but he still couldn't help but wonder if his feelings weren't those of someone taking advantage of someone else. He didn't think he was taking advantage of Cal, but now that the seed was planted, he couldn't help but question his motives.

Travis needed to speak to Mikael. His friend and boss would be objective and tell him straight out if Travis' doubts were valid. As he stepped out of the shower and dried off on his way to his bedroom, he had every intention to call Mikael once he settled on his bed.

Mikael and Adam wouldn't be asleep and due to the early morning hour, Travis normally wouldn't bother them. However, he was really disturbed over the thought he had in the shower and knew Mikael would understand his need to talk.

He'd just sat on the edge of his bed when he realized his phone was still in the back pocket of his jeans which were now in a crumpled pile of clothes on his bathroom floor. Travis sighed and stood to retrieve his phone. He picked his jeans up off the floor when his phone dinged to notify him of a text message.

Hope rose in his chest. No one in his family sent him text messages at this time of day. If there were an emergency, they would call. So, his heart rate increased as he swiped the screen and opened his phone's messenger app.

Cal: *Thank you for tonight.*

Travis couldn't help the smile that spread his lips. All thoughts of calling Mikael disappeared at seeing Cal's name on his screen.

Travis: *You are most welcome, beautiful. Thank you for joining me.*

Several seconds passed which felt long enough that Travis didn't think Cal was going to reply before he actually did.

Cal: *You were right.*

Travis frowned because he had no idea what Cal was referring to. So, all he could do was ask.

Travis: *About what, pretty?*

Cal: *Never having been on a date before.*

Travis: *I'm glad I was your first then.*

Cal: *My first... My...*

Travis looked at his screen and waited for more as he lay back on his bed. He adjusted his pillows and caught Cal's scent from when he'd slept on the bed. The smell permeated Travis' senses and he couldn't help but close his eyes and breathe deep. Finally, he sighed and opened his eyes to look at his phone. It appeared Cal wasn't going to finish his sentence without prompting.

Travis: *Your what?*

Cal: *Well.*

Travis waited.

Cal: *It's embarrassing. I shouldn't have said anything.*

Travis: *You don't need to be embarrassed with me. I wish I wouldn't have made you feel that way.*

Cal: *You didn't.*

Cal's reply was so fast Travis felt reassured he hadn't done anything to make Cal feel uncomfortable or embarrassed. In fact, he replayed their date in his mind and couldn't find a single instance to cause Cal embarrassment.

Travis: *Why are you embarrassed then, sweetie?*

Cal: *I've never been kissed before. I mean. I've done stuff. Had sex. But never been kissed so it's embarrassing. Oh God, I'm rambling!*

Travis laughed. He couldn't help it even if he was somewhat shocked Cal had never even been kissed before.

Travis: *I'm glad I was your first for that, too.*

Travis: *Did you enjoy your first kiss?*

The long pause before Cal replied had Travis questioning if he should've kissed Cal at all. Travis almost didn't ask Cal for a good night kiss after he made the comment about his dating history. However, he just couldn't not ask, so he did. He resisted kissing Cal the way he desired and was purposely restrained. Purposely gentle.

Cal: *Yes, very much.*

Cal's text snapped Travis out of his doubts over asking Cal for a kiss. He was starting to think Cal only said yes because of some sense that was what he was required to do at the end of the date. It was a relief that wasn't the case. Travis was about to reply when his phone dinged again.

Cal: *More than I should probably admit.*

Travis: *Why is that?*

Travis: *You can tell me anything, you know.*

Travis: *Did my kiss turn you on?*

Travis sent his follow-up question before he even thought it might compound Cal's embarrassment. He was distracted by the thought that his kiss turned Cal on. It turned Travis on and he couldn't help but hope the same could be said for Cal.

Cal: *It did. A lot.*

Cal: *But you're sexy as hell and turn me on anyway. Just watching you work... Feeling you pet me... God, I'm doing it again. Sorry.*

Travis didn't think Cal had a damn thing to be sorry about. Just seeing Cal's words on his screen verifying the beautiful garoul was *actually* as attracted to him as much as he was to Cal, flooded him with warmth and made his dick twitch.

Travis: *Never apologize for how you feel. I'm glad you find me as sexy as I find you, beautiful.*

Travis: *What did you do when you got home?*

Travis dared to type and held his breath waiting for a reply. He normally wouldn't restrain himself from going after what or who he wanted aggressively. But there was just something about Cal that made Travis want to romance the hell out of the man. He wanted more than just a quick fuck. It was a feeling he hadn't felt in more than two centuries and almost didn't recognize.

Travis was more than sure Cal needing help or his now confirmed innocence had nothing to do with his feelings, either. There was just something about the calico bobtail garoul that made Travis feel things he hadn't felt in a long, long time.

Cal: *Well, I was turned on. A lot. So, I...*

Travis: *You what?*

Cal: *I touched myself thinking it was you touching me.*

Travis inhaled so sharply between his teeth that it sounded like a hiss in the quiet of his bedroom. His mind had no problem, absolutely no fucking problem, visualizing Cal touching himself. He could clearly picture Cal's slim fingers wrapping around his cock and stroking. The visual, along with Cal's words clearly stated what he'd been imagining, his fingers, his hand, made Travis instantly hard. It took everything he had not to stroke his suddenly throbbing cock so he could reply to Cal's text.

Travis: *You don't know what telling me that has just done to me.*

Cal: *I'm sorry.*

Travis could almost feel Cal retreating from embarrassment or the thought he should never have admitted anything because Travis might be offended. He needed to clarify that shit right now. So, he did.

Travis: *I'm not. Don't you dare be, either.*

Travis*: I'm glad to know it's not just me who gets hard when we are together.*

Travis already knew that wasn't the case since he smelled Cal's arousal earlier. Still, hearing the beautiful blonde admit as much even via a text message only made Travis fill with warmth once more.

Travis: *I wish I had been there. To see you touching yourself.*

Travis: *It's probably good I wasn't, though.*

Cal: *Why?*

Travis didn't think Cal understood the extent to which he was turned on. Just the fact he was now only holding and texting with one hand so his other could stroke his cock was proof enough. Of course, Cal wasn't here to see his current state, but that didn't make his current level of arousal any less.

Travis: *Because I don't think I would be able to just watch without having a taste.*

Texting one-handed was a bitch, but the slow strokes on his cock which caused just enough friction to keep him on edge made it so worth the effort.

Cal: *You want to taste me?*

Cal: *Just what would you taste?*

"Fuck," Travis cursed into his empty bedroom. He could hear Cal's voice in his mind asking those questions as if the sexy man were whispering in his ear.

Travis: *You. All of you.*

Travis: *Texting you now is HARD.*

Sending replies to Cal wasn't the only thing hard as his cock in the palm of his hand could attest to. Travis could easily get off right this moment if he wanted to, but the building anticipation for whatever Cal might text next made him hold back the pleasure of his release. He was looking at the open text message screen of his phone and holding it in one hand so tight he instinctively knew any more pressure would break the fucker while stroking his aching cock with his other hand.

The damn thing rang. Travis actually startled. Startled so bad he released his cock and used both hands to catch his cell phone which he dropped. Once in hand, Cal's name was clearly displayed on the screen. He didn't hesitate to answer the call even though Cal calling him *right now* was the last damn thing he expected. Travis forced his breath to steady before he answered.

"Hi."

"Hi."

Cal's voice sounded soft and almost sleepy. The man should be asleep after the long night they'd had, but that was only a fleeting thought for Travis. He was too absorbed with how Cal sounded, as if he was about to drift off or as if he'd just woken up. Too suddenly absorbed with what it would feel like hearing Cal's voice like this caress his skin.

"You should be sleeping." Travis made sure Cal could hear the smile in his tone which matched the one spreading his lips.

"I would say you should be too, but," Cal paused because he didn't have to say what they both knew. "Plus, you said texting was *hard*, so I thought it might be easier if we just talked."

Travis couldn't have stopped his moan even if he wanted to. The way Cal emphasized 'hard' was more than enough to let Travis know Cal may have not been very experienced, but he sure as hell wasn't as innocent as he appeared.

"Is it *hard* to talk to me?"

Travis heard the emphasis on 'hard' again, but he also heard the hesitation and insecurity in Cal's voice. The last thing Travis ever wanted was for Cal to feel hesitant or insecure with him. Never with him.

"No. It's just *hard*. Period," Travis replied softly.

"I'm sorry," Cal apologized again although Travis had no idea why.

"Never be sorry for how you make me feel, beautiful. I'm not."

"Maybe I should've come home with you. Then neither of us would have this problem," Cal whispered.

Travis put his phone on speaker and set it down. It took a moment for his lust fogged mind to realize what Cal said. The pretty garoul had already admitted to getting off when he got home, but apparently Cal was just as aroused again as Travis was at this moment.

"Maybe you should have," Travis agreed before he continued. "But I don't think dating actually works that way. Don't get me wrong, beautiful. There is nothing

I want more right this moment than to feel your perfect naked body flush with mine."

The moan that echoed from Travis' cell phone speaker was sinful. So sinful, Travis couldn't wait to feel it again more times against his skin. The sound so distracted Travis that he totally lost track of what he had been saying.

"I thought of that earlier," Cal continued to whisper. "I'm thinking of that now. Lying in your bed. Next to you." Cal was breathing hard and Travis had no problem imagining his chest heaving and flushed with desire and want.

"My bed still smells like you." Travis stroked himself steadily. It wouldn't take much for him to cum. "Your scent is surrounding me and all I can think of is how much stronger it would be if you were here under me."

"Oh, God," Cal breathed out harshly and he sounded like a choir of angels singing to Travis' ears.

"Would you like that, beautiful? Me on top of you, treating you like the precious treasure you are while I make love to you."

The long drawn out groan from his cell phone filled Travis' bedroom and told him everything he needed to know about the effect his words had on Cal. They weren't empty words and Travis hoped Cal didn't think he said them just to get Cal off because that sure as shit wasn't the case.

However, hearing Cal's ragged breaths while he flew high from his orgasm was more than enough to make Travis forget everything about what Cal might think of what he'd said. Just hearing the sounds of Cal experience relief and panting harshly into his phone was more than enough to send Travis over the edge into his own bliss.

Nothing but harsh breaths filled Travis' bedroom. Cal's. His. They were both breathing hard. Travis couldn't wait until he could actually see Cal's chest heave, his skin flushed with pleasure, and sweat beading all over his fair skin just so he could lick up every drop.

There was no telling how long Travis listened to his breathing along with Cal's through his phone. But, eventually silence settled around him again. Cal was so quiet Travis actually checked his phone to ensure they were still connected. They were.

"Are you okay, beautiful," Travis asked quietly.

"You keep calling me that. Why?"

It took a moment for Cal to reply, but when he did Travis could only smile and answer honestly. "Because you are." Travis had no problem hearing Cal's snort of disbelief. "You are the most beautiful man I've ever met, Calvin."

There was a long pause before Cal replied, "oh."

"Thank you for tonight," Travis said and was sure Cal understood he wasn't just talking about their sexy texting an impromptu phone sex.

"I had a good time too, Travis."

"Will I see you at the Brew tonight?" Travis couldn't help but ask.

There was no hesitation in Cal's reply and that made Travis' heart soar. "Yeah, I'll be in."

"I'll see you then. Sleep well, Cal."

"I will. See you tonight."

The call disconnected and for the first time in a long time Travis wished he slept if for no other reason than to make the time seem to go faster before he could see Cal again.

Chapter Thirteen

Cal was initially embarrassed when he saw Travis at The Witch's Brew that night. However, Travis didn't treat him any different after they'd essentially had phone sex. No, Travis greeted him as he always had: with a smile, a wink, and a wave of a water bottle held in his hand to verify that's what Cal was drinking.

"Glad you came in," Travis smiled and once again Cal was struck by just how sexy this man was.

"I said I would." Cal returned Travis' smile.

"Never doubted you, beautiful." Travis shot him another wink. "It's busy tonight, but just wave me down when you're ready for another." Travis nodded toward the bottle of water Cal held.

"Will do. Go, get to work." Cal grinned and watched Travis' sexy as hell body work his way down the bar to serve customers.

Travis brought him three more bottles of water without him asking over the next two hours. Cal was drinking the water while he watched Travis work. He could watch the hot man sling drinks all night long. Travis flirted with his customers, both male and female, but it seemed superficial compared to how Travis interacted with him. Cal was reassured he could tell the difference.

It was slightly after one a.m. when Cal noticed Mikael's long blonde haired head moving through the crowd in his direction. Mikael was taking his time and seemed to glide through the crowd. He discreetly removed the hands of men and women who tried to stop him with their advances. Mikael finally stopped next to him and Cal offered the owner of the club a friendly smile.

"Glad to see you back again, Calvin."

"You have a nice club," Cal complimented since he didn't do so when he originally found out Mikael owned The Witch's Brew.

"Thank you." Mikael smiled. "I don't think you are here for my club anymore, though." Mikael gave him a knowing grin and Cal felt his cheeks heat slightly. "It's okay. If my employee and friend wasn't like a brother, I would be here to watch him work as well. Oh, and the fact that my other half, Adam," Mikael nodded toward the huge ass man who'd retrieved a chair for him last night and was standing at the railing of the second-floor balcony like a gargoyle perched on a chapel overlooking everything. "Wouldn't appreciate my attention being elsewhere. Not that it would be."

"He's big," Cal said and immediately slapped his hand over his mouth.

Mikael laughed. "That he is."

The way Mikael said those words and the glint in his eyes sent Cal's mind straight to the gutter. And, of course, his mental visual of the attractive blonde standing next to him and the large security guy who was the owner's boyfriend naked, intertwined together, made Cal feel his cheeks heat up even more.

Cal wasn't a prude. Sheltered, yes, but not a prude. No one his age as far as he was concerned could be a prude with how easily accessible porn was on the Internet. Still, not being a prude didn't mean he could control what caused him to blush. In fact, Cal was pretty sure he'd blushed more since coming to The Witch's Brew the first time, and especially since meeting Travis, then he had in his entire life combined before coming to Chicago.

"Let us know if you need anything." Mikael squeezed Cal's shoulder before he disappeared back into the crowd.

Cal wasn't sure what to make of the owner's offer. So, he gave Mikael's words no more thought since his full bladder decided to make itself known.

Cal left his half-empty bottle of water on the bar top he'd claimed as his space and started the process of moving through the crowd toward the restrooms. His progress was slowed, to a stop more often than not, when he sensed the predator garouls who either worked in the club or were just out to have a good time. He finally made it to the men's room and didn't sense any predators behind him or in the bathroom once he stepped inside.

Cal forced himself to breathe out a sigh of relief. He'd only sense two garouls who weren't obvious employees of the club. They had been far enough away from him when he sensed them, they hadn't even turned in his direction, and so he felt safe entering the bathroom to take a piss. Cal should've known better than to think however safe he felt didn't equate to how safe he *actually* was when it came to sensing predators.

He was just zipping up his jeans when the bathroom door opened and the space was filled with PREDATOR. Instinctively, Cal stepped back. The man himself was unremarkable. Shaggy brown hair and brown eyes which would likely turn amber or golden depending on his shifted form were his most noticeable features. He was attractive by Cal's standards. The guy was wearing clothes that showed enough skin to entice anyone who was looking for a hook-up.

The guy was shorter than Cal by a few inches, but he was just as muscular as Travis. The reality was Cal could've not given less of a shit to how the guy looked in his human form. It was the predator vibe which crawled over him like a physical touch and the hungry look in the guy's eyes that caused Cal to be concerned. There was nowhere for Cal to go. The predator blocked his escape.

"Well, hello pretty kitty," the guy cooed casually and Cal couldn't stop the warning hiss that escaped his throat.

It was a low hiss-like growl sound which would've echoed off the walls had the club music not been so loud. The guy recognized he was a feline, so Cal knew he was either a larger feline or a garoul who was something which didn't fear cats at all. He didn't have the brain capacity at the moment to figure out which that could be.

"Ahh, kitty, kitty," the guy practically tutted while he stepped closer. "Don't be like that, now." The guy was less than two feet away and still *talking*. "I just want to play. Play with the kitty, kitty."

By the time the guy was half a foot from him Cal's fear and panic crested to the point where his feline took control. He shifted and backed into the wall behind him. His back arched and he hissed in warning.

"Dude," the guy said almost casually. It was clear he hadn't expected Cal to shift, but that didn't stop him from continuing his approach. "C'mere, kitty."

The asshole predator squatted down and reached out to grab him. Cal didn't hesitate to bat a clawed paw at the asshole's hand. He connected and knew he drew blood by the guy's harsh curse.

Cal didn't think the predator would shift, but the guy didn't have to if he wanted to hurt Cal. And, apparently that was his intention since he reached out for Cal again. Once more Cal swiped at him, but it wasn't enough to prevent the asshole from grabbing him and picking him up. Cal screeched, twisted, and attempted to claw himself free. Several times his claws drew blood on the asshole's face and hands, but the guy just wouldn't let go.

It didn't matter that Cal had no way to escape, he couldn't run out into the club, but at least he would be *free*. Cal's yowls and screeching echoed off the bathroom walls and were all he heard even though the predator was cursing up a storm. He didn't care. He just wanted to be *let go* and feel the cool tile underneath his paws.

The sound of the restroom door slamming open never even registered in Cal's mind. One moment, he was struggling to be free, clawing at anything and everything he could get his paws on and yowling as if he were being tortured. The next, he was free. He landed on his feet and darted into the closest stall.

Cal cowered behind the toilet and watched the stall doorway. He was ready to bolt again at the first sign of anyone approaching him. There wasn't far he could go since there was no way he could open the restroom door in this form, but there were three stalls and three urinals which he was more than sure he could use to his advantage in order not to be caught by the predator again.

His ears twitched forward and he forced himself to focus on what he heard instead of the sound of his pounding heart in his ears or his panting breath.

Everything was quiet. Eerily quiet. The only sound was the muted bass of the club's music. Not hearing anything didn't cause Cal to relax at all. No, he knew better than to think silence equated safety.

Feline's stalked their prey silently and Cal was aware wolves did the same. Most prey didn't even know they were targeted by a predator until they were dying or lucky enough to sense them and flee. So, no, Cal didn't relax at all even though he forced his heaving chest and racing heart to settle. He was hyperaware, his adrenaline spiking through the roof, so he had no concept of time. The bathroom could've been quiet for five minutes, or five seconds. His reaction to the bathroom door opening would have been the same, regardless.

He was huddled into such a ball behind the toilet that Cal only allowed one eye to stare at the cracked open stall door. He may have been hunched and ready to bolt, but he didn't. Instead he growled in warning, the sound coming from low in his chest, the moment he saw a shadow across the floor.

"Hey, it's okay. I'm here to help you."

A voice Cal didn't recognize reached his ears before the body attached to the shadow pushed the stall door open all the way. Cal issued another low warning growl. It didn't matter to him that the thin guy who stood to the side of the now open stall door wore a bright neon yellow security T-shirt and looked harmless. It didn't matter that Cal recognized him as a life drinker like Travis and Mikael, either.

"He's gone. We kicked him out," the security guy said softly. "I'll wait out here and you can shift. Okay?"

The security guy stepped out of view, but Cal still didn't move from his hiding place. He had no intention to do so anytime soon, either. The silence in the restroom stretched on and was only broken by the security guy telling people trying to get in that the restroom was currently out of order. Cal should have felt reassured the security guy was keeping people away, but he wasn't.

"Adam." The guy saying a name randomly after a few moments made Cal's hackles rise from uncertainty over what might happen next. "I don't think they are going to come out let alone shift back... Yeah, they aren't happy at being kept out... Yeah. Okay. Thanks."

The club goers who needed the men's room weren't happy. *To fucking bad*, Cal thought uncharitably. Cal's hearing was sensitive enough to hear the other side of the security guy's conversation. This Adam person was coming to the restroom and would relieve this guy and handle the situation once he got here. Cal wasn't sure how he felt about someone saying they would 'handle' the situation which was basically him.

The bathroom door opened, a loud blast of club music entering, before it closed again. It was clear to Cal the previous security guy left and now the other security person had taken his place. Cal didn't move. He didn't take his gaze off the open stall door, either. He saw the man's shadow before he saw the man. A low growl rumbled in his chest even though he recognized the big ass security guy who now stood a few feet away from the open stall door.

"It's okay, Cal."

Cal wasn't so sure about that even though the guy used his name and Cal recognized the huge man as Mikael's boyfriend. His rumbling growl continued in warning.

"I'm Adam." The guy sat down on the dirty bathroom tiled floor. He crossed his legs and relaxed his hands over his ankles. "I saw Mikael talking to you, so I'm sure you know he's my boyfriend. I've also seen you here to see Travis and how he looks at you. You mean something to him. Anyone that means something to someone in our family means something to me, too."

Cal poked his head out further from behind the toilet. He thought he had meant something to Travis, but not enough that Travis had talked about him to his friends or family as both Mikael and now Adam claimed they were.

"I understand if you don't want to shift back yet. That's okay," Adam said softly enough that Cal was sure if his hearing weren't so sensitive, he wouldn't have heard the man at all. "Let me take you up to our apartment until you are ready to go back to the club or go home."

Cal hesitantly took two steps out from behind the toilet. He understood he couldn't remain hidden here all night. He wasn't a large garoul, but even the drunkest norm would notice a calico bobtail hiding behind a toilet.

"I promise you will be safe in our apartment and I'll let Travis know you're there as soon as I get you up there."

The mention of Travis' name seemed to encourage Cal to come completely out of hiding. It didn't hurt that he talked with Mikael the night before and also knew this large and admittedly scary man was Mikael's boyfriend. Slowly, Cal crept toward Adam and was extremely cautious of the man's behavior. Adam didn't move a muscle. The man's hands remained relaxed atop his ankles even when Cal was within grabbing distance.

Cautiously, Cal continued forward until he was close enough to head butt the large man's hand. He was ready to leap back but Adam still didn't move. Cal stepped back and looked up into the man's almost grass green eyes. Adam's gaze held the same sincerity, caring, and concern Cal was used to seeing in Travis' mesmerizing look every time the sexy bartender's eyes met his.

"C'mon. Let me take you upstairs and you can wait for the club to close and Travis to get off work."

Cal stepped forward again and pushed his head against Adam's hand at the same time he rested a paw on Adams booted foot.

"I'll take that as permission to take you upstairs."

Adam smiled, but still didn't move to touch him. Cal purred his agreement and stepped further onto Adam's booted feet. Both of his white covered paws rested on Adams boots and he pushed his head harder against Adam's lax hand.

"Okay. I'm going to shadow step us up there so we don't have to go through the club. I'm not sure if you know what that means and I really hope you won't freak out, but I'm going to pick you up, kill the lights, and then we will be in our apartment upstairs. If this works for you, crawl up into my lap."

Adam slowly moved his hands to the sides to give Cal access to his lap. Cal didn't hesitate to move into the space between Adam's thick thighs. Adam breathed out a sigh before Cal felt one of his huge hands wrap around his belly. Adam pulled him close to his chest and held him snugly before he pushed up from the floor with his other hand. Three steps brought them to the light switch which Adam instantly flicked off.

The club restroom was plunged into darkness. Cal never felt them shadow step as seemed to be a life drinkers' way of travel before light surrounded them again. They were in a different bathroom now and Cal knew that had he not experienced the shock of ending up somewhere different after the lights went out and came on again, he would've totally freaked out. Freaked out like he had when Travis took him home. The way Adam was currently holding him made Cal suspect the man was expecting just that sort of reaction.

"Meow," was all Cal could offer to let Adam know he was okay.

Adam chuckled and opened the bathroom door. Cal didn't struggle to get down while Adam carried him further into the apartment. If he trusted the scary large man to get him out of the club's restroom, he trusted the man not to hurt him now.

"Putting you down now," Adam informed before he bent over the back of a couch and laid Cal down. "Make yourself at home. There's food if you're hungry and stuff to drink in the fridge."

Adam started walking toward the door Cal assumed would take him back down to the club even though he couldn't hear a hint of bass from the music he knew was still blasting downstairs. Adam turned back after he opened the door.

"If you decide you want to go home," Adam started and Cal heard no judgment one way or the other in his tone. "Just leave through here. Exit through the door in the next room and that will put you in a hall that leads to the balcony of the club. I'm sure you can find your way from there."

"Meow," Cal replied the only way he could while in this form.

Adam nodded, but stared at him for a few more moments as if weighing if he should say something more or not. Adam seemed to make up his mind because he spoke again. "I hope you'll stay here until the club closes. Mikael would like that, as well. We haven't told Travis what happened yet."

"Meow?"

Adam seemed to hear the question in his feline response. "We don't want him to worry or freak out because you could have been hurt. There is nothing more deadly than a possessive life drinker who wants to protect the one they love." Adam paused. "So, we hope you will stay here until the club closes and Travis' is done for the night. But if you want to go, you are free to do so." With those words, Adam stepped through the door and closed it behind him.

Cal curled in on himself. His back legs were pulled up close to his head and his front legs overlapped them while he turned his head to the side and stared at the ceiling. Cal knew from seeing pictures of domestic cats online that some norms were bothered or even disturbed on how his current position could be comfortable at all. But it was. However, Cal's current position, snuggled in a ball on the soft leather couch cushions, wasn't even a blip on his thought radar. No, Adam's words were swirling chaotically in his head to the point they felt like a pinball and his brain was the bumpers.

Just what did he mean? Life drinkers were obviously deadly. They drank blood for Christ sake. But the whole thing about protecting one they love? What was that all about?

Cal hadn't known Travis or Travis him long enough for love to even be a thing. *Right?* Then again, Cal had never been in love. Sure, he knew what it felt like to love someone. He loved his mother. He even loved his father before the man decided Cal needed to die. Cal had loved Abe, too. But Cal had never known the type of love he'd seen on TV or in movies, so maybe Travis being in love with him was possible even though they hadn't known each other that long. It was that thought which bounced around in his mind until he finally drifted off into a doze.

Chapter Fourteen

Initially, panic threatened to rule Travis when he realized Cal was gone for way longer than he should have been to take a piss. His panic only increased when Chris gave a situation report of something happening in the men's room involving garouls. He was briefly tempted to follow his concern for Cal and jump over the bar to head in that direction. However, as much as his gut told him Cal was one of the garouls involved, Travis trusted his family enough to take care of his beautiful small garoul.

Still, the trust he had in his family who worked security didn't relieve his stress until he heard Chris call the all clear and request Adam's presence in the restroom. Adam hadn't directly interacted with Cal, but was Mikael's boyfriend. Travis was sure, at least he thought he was, that Mikael would have shared that information and pointed out his lover. Even if Mikael hadn't, Travis had to take assurance that at least Cal would recognize Adam as a life drinker like him.

However, as Travis robotically took drink orders, filled them, and took payments, his mind was focused on the men's room and the line that only grew longer. Adam and Cal were inside, he was sure. He was just about to key up his earpiece when Mikael appeared before him across the bar.

"Adam is taking care of him," his longtime friend and boss informed him.

Travis could only trust Mikael's words since he heard nothing over their security comms after Adam entered the men's room. Mikael wouldn't lie to him. He had no reason to and Travis surely had no reason to doubt Mikael's words.

"Okay," Travis begrudgingly replied.

"Adam will get him to our apartment," Mikael said with such certainty Travis couldn't doubt him even if he wanted to. "Finish the night. There's only an hour left then come upstairs."

All Travis managed to do was nod. He understood full well how Mikael felt about their family and he knew full well the lengths Mikael would and had gone to in order to keep them all safe. It was only Travis' two centuries worth of this knowledge since meeting Mikael which allowed him to finish the last hour of work.

His mind was steadfastly on Cal while his body moved through the motions of serving drinks and taking payments. Muscle memory was a wonderful thing at times because Travis was more than sure if he hadn't been working in taverns, inns, and clubs for the last hundred years he'd be fucked right now. Still, doing his job by rote didn't stop him from feeling the time drag by. Every second felt like a minute and every minute felt like an hour.

BT announced last call and Travis filled the diehards drink orders as he done hundreds of times before, but the moment the house lights came on he was heading toward the stairs. The only way to get to Mikael's apartment without shadow stepping directly was to cross the upper balcony, enter the hall which led to Mikael's office, and let himself in through the door Mikael didn't permit many to enter.

Travis' key card barely registered to turn the lock to the hallway green before Travis was moving. There was no threat that norms would see him here, so he didn't hesitate to use his life drinker ability to move fast. He was down the hall, through Mikael's office, and into his friend and boss' apartment within the blink of an eye.

Travis wasn't sure what to expect when he arrived in Mikael's apartment even though his friend and Adam both assured him Cal would be there. Having that assurance was comforting, but comforting to his heart or not, Travis didn't know if he was about to find a terrified man or an equally terrified calico bobtail. He found neither. Cal laid, almost an impossible ball, on Mikael's leather couch. Once Travis calmed his heart and breath, he could easily see Cal was sleeping. Well, maybe not sleeping but at least dozing restfully.

Slowly and as silently as only a life drinker could achieve, Travis approached Mikael's couch. He sat down as close as he dared to Cal so not to wake him. Just seeing the small garoul curled up and safe on Mikael's couch lifted the weight of fear off his chest he had never expected to have for the man. Feeling that fear subside, Travis reached out and gently ran his fingers over Cal's soft fur.

Heat pressed against Cal's spine and the gentle sensation of being pet slithered through his mind. He loved it when Abe woke him this way. Cal tensed his body, stretching all four of his legs straight out and arched his head around and back in search of more of the touch which made him feel so good. So, loved. He finally relaxed his legs and twisted to curl onto his back, front paws in the air and head turned toward where Abe had been petting him.

Abe's warm palm moved to his chest and Cal moved his curled paws to the side so he could enjoy more of Abe's loving caresses. His purrs came naturally from pure contentment. He was safe with Abe for the time being, so Cal promised himself he would enjoy every moment possible when Abe showed him affection and he could offer Abe comfort in return.

Cal squirmed on his back and brought his paws to the side of Abe's wrist. His claws remained retracted and he wasn't really grasping Abe's wrist, but more holding on to ensure the man wouldn't stop running his fingers through the fur on his chest.

"You are so beautiful."

Cal purred in response. He could do nothing else because Abe made him feel so good. But wait. That wasn't Abe's old tobacco graveled voice he just heard. Abe never called him beautiful, either. Abe always called him his 'lucky cat.'

"My little lucky cat" Abe used to say while he rubbed Cal's chest and stomach. Never beautiful. Always 'lucky cat.'

Slowly, Cal opened his eyes and forced himself to wake up more. He didn't look down at the hand which was attached to the fingers and were curling in gentle circles through the fur on his chest. No, his gaze traveled up the arm to the man the hand was attached to. Stunning dark gray eyes, which were doing a piss poor job of hiding concern, met his gaze.

Travis. Not Abe. Travis.

Cal wiggled enough to be more fully on his back. He couldn't describe the heartache he felt at realizing it wasn't Abe who petted him with so much familiarity. He also couldn't describe the relief he felt at seeing Travis.

At feeling Travis' touch and knowing it was his hand, his fingers, which were caressing him so soothingly.

Travis smiled down at Cal while Cal's paws seemed to wrap around his wrist to prevent him from discontinuing the petting he was giving the garoul. He had no intentions to stop rubbing Cal's chest until the stunning multicolored garoul indicated in some way or another he should. So, instead Travis peered into the seafoam green eyes which finally opened more than just a crack.

The vibration Travis felt under his palm from Cal's gentle purring shot another bolt of warmth straight through him. As wrong as it seemed, and surely was, feeling Cal's pleasure from his touch while Cal was in his garoul form aroused the hell out of Travis. He had no desire to do anything sexual while Cal was in his bobtail form, but there was just something arousing about knowing he was giving Cal pleasure from just the gentlest of touches.

"I could stay like this with you forever, though I am sure Mikael and Adam would grow wary of me staying on their couch just to be near you," Travis whispered softly and curled his fingers once more into the soft fur on Cal's chest.

Cal could stay here forever, too. Travis' hot palm resting on his belly and his fingers systematically curling into the fur on his chest made Cal never want to move again. However, he understood as much as he wanted to just lay here, twist, and bend his body around to feel more of Travis' heat, he couldn't. Staying on Mikael's couch wouldn't be fair to anyone. Not to Mikael and Adam who lived here and certainly not to Travis who had a home of his own to go to after a night of working at the club. Of course, staying in his feline form wasn't fair to him, either, even if the last thing he wanted to do right now was shift back. Travis' hand caressing him felt just too damn good, but they couldn't stay here.

Travis startled when Cal moved. One moment, Cal was on his back, body practically shaped like a U with his paws bracketing Travis' wrist. The next, Cal was on his feet. Cal didn't bolt away from him, but Travis was sure Cal's reaction had everything to do with what he just said.

"I didn't mean we needed to move right now." Travis reached out a palm toward Cal's head.

Cal didn't hesitate to walk directly into Travis' palm. He head butted the hand held out to him, before he took turns rubbing his cheeks, his scent glands, along both sides of Travis' hand. Cal purred continuously while he rubbed his head against Travis' hand and his purr only grew louder when Travis' fingers scratched behind his ears, along his nose, and under his chin.

It was obvious to Travis Cal was enjoying the attention he was giving him. However, it was just as obvious from Cal's reaction to his benign comment that regardless how good Travis was currently making him feel, the small garoul was uncomfortable staying here much longer.

"I want to take you home with me again. You can leave after you wake up like you did before, but if you don't want to, I understand. If that's the case, then please shift and I will call you a ride."

Cal didn't think for a moment Travis would treat him any differently if he chose to shift and leave. That wasn't what Cal wanted to do, so he didn't hesitate to step onto Travis' lap.

"I guess that means you want to come home with me again, huh?"

"Meow," Cal rumbled an answered and pressed his head up beneath Travis' chin. Travis' almost delightful chuckle would've made Cal smile if his feline muzzle could form such an expression. He couldn't smile, though, so instead he purred louder.

"Okay, beautiful." Travis ran his hand down Cal's back. "I'm going to pick you up then we will head home."

Cal didn't resist Travis when the sexy man picked him up. If anything, Cal attempted to snuggle closer as Travis pressed him close to his chest when they walked toward Mikael's darkened bathroom.

"We're home, beautiful," Travis informed Cal as he opened his bathroom door.

Cal didn't seem in any hurry to escape his embrace, so Travis walked them both over to his bed. He sat down and turned just enough to lay Cal down. The slight prick of claws through his T-shirt on his chest wasn't enough to hurt. However, they were enough to convey Cal had no desire to be set down on the bed.

"I was going to get us something to eat," Travis informed the soft bundle of fur he held.

Cal wasn't hungry, so he flexed his paws again just enough his claws stabbed through Travis' T-shirt. He didn't push his claws out far. Just enough to get Travis' attention.

Travis chuckled. "Okay, okay. No food then."

Travis positioned himself on his bed so he was resting his head on his pillow, but almost against his headboard, as well. He wanted to be able to watch Cal, since Cal didn't seem to want to lie on his bed. So, Travis got comfortable.

Cal stretched out on Travis' muscular chest and stomach. He wasn't a large cat. However, his head still rested on Travis' pec and his back paws reached just below Travis' waistband. Cal wouldn't even take up that much space if he weren't stretched out on his side. Travis' arm was wrapped along his back and his hand cupped Cal's back paws. His other hand slowly petted him from ears to the tail he was missing. Cal purred his pleasure loudly.

"Get some sleep, love," Travis whispered.

Cal *was* beginning to doze off, but Travis calling him love snapped him back awake. He craned his head back to look at Travis. It didn't matter that his view of the man's face was upside down and shaded in grays and blues.

"I'm sorry, baby." Travis smiled softly. "Didn't mean to wake you if you were drifting off. Relax and get some rest, beautiful."

Travis' hand never stopped caressing him even though Cal changed the angle of his head. Travis' touch felt wonderful, almost as good as hearing him call Cal beautiful again. Cal was starting to love hearing Travis call him beautiful even though Travis was the more attractive of the two of them, by far. Cal returned his head to rest on Travis' chest and pushed all thoughts from his mind except for the steady beat in his ears which was Travis' heart.

Cal continued to purr under his stroking hand even though Travis recognized the slow and steady beat of Cal's heart which told him Cal had drifted off to sleep. He was amused Cal still made that soft rumble. Travis didn't really know much about cats. Large or small. Garoul or those in the wild. He would have to correct that void in his knowledge. So far, it seemed he was reading Cal well while the small garoul was in his feline form. Still, he wanted to know everything there was to know about Cal in either form.

Travis was hungry and not for food. He could wait a while longer to have a meal, though. Cal was relaxed enough that he was resting all of his feline weight in the crook of the arm Travis had wrapped around him. Travis was sure if he moved his arm, Cal would slide right off him and onto the bed. Cal would probably freak out from the upset of his current balance, too. The last thing Travis wanted to do was startle Cal awake, especially since he'd finally fell asleep.

So, as gently as Travis could, he slowly moved his arm which currently supported Cal's weight. He rolled his body at the same time he lowered his arm to the bed. The movement put Cal on his back and his claws pierced Travis' T-shirt again. Travis froze thinking he'd awoken Cal. He hadn't, so he assumed Cal extending his claws was an unconscious reaction on the small garoul's part.

Travis rested his forearm over Cal's body before he moved his other arm to bend under his head. Cal twisted his body slightly until his head was almost in Travis' armpit. Travis wanted to chuckle at how adorable Cal was while moving in his sleep, but he repressed the sound and opted to smile instead. He didn't need to sleep, so he watched Cal for a while before just closing his eyes to rest.

Cal felt a delicious weight over his middle and holding him close to a warm body. He didn't need to open his eyes to know it was Travis who held him so intimately even if he was in his feline form. Still, now that he was awake Cal couldn't resist stretching all four of his legs straight out and he tilted his head back far enough to see Travis' face. He expected to meet Travis' stunning steel gray eyes, especially since all four of his paws effectively seemed to push the man away when he stretched. Instead, Cal looked upon Travis' sleeping features. Travis seemed to be even more attractive while asleep.

That can't be right. He said he doesn't sleep.

Cal's feline brows crinkled in the closest expression to a frown he could make in this form. Still, he froze. He didn't want to wake the sexy bartender up if he was indeed sleeping. However, he couldn't resist touching Travis with one of his paws. At first, he just tapped the man's chest with a padded paw. He did it a few more times, before he finally rested his paw on the hard muscle of Travis' chest.

Travis quietly moaned to warn Cal. He didn't want to speak and startle the pretty garoul. Travis wasn't concerned about Cal scratching the hell out of him if the garoul was startled. No, he just didn't want to send another bolt of fear through the man. Cal had felt more fear in the last twenty-four hours than anyone should feel a hundred years.

"You're so snuggly," Travis rumbled.

Cal would've laughed if he could; instead, he made a pitiful chuff-like sound which was usually heard only in tigers and reached out with a paw to touch Travis' chin.

"Is that your way of laughing at me?" Travis opened his eyes and tilted his head down to better look at Cal.

"Meow," Cal issued to confirm Travis' assumption.

His paw slipped off Travis' chin when the life drinker tilted his head down to look more fully into his eyes. Cal met Travis' incredibly gray, almost silver in the low light of the bedroom, eyes. His gaze was fond. Cal would almost venture that what he was seeing was love, but he had never known love and pushed the wishful thinking from his mind.

"Are you hungry? I am and can make you something to eat."

Travis smiled softly down at him. Cal lifted a paw and pressed the pads against Travis' lips. It was the only way he could think of to tell Travis to shut the hell up while he twisted to get closer to the heat of Travis' body.

"Okay, beautiful. We can lay here as long as you want." Travis scooted Cal closer against him. "I'm not in a hurry to go anywhere. I can have my meal later."

Travis mentioning eating for the third time since they've returned to Travis' house reminded Cal food wasn't where the life drinkers got their nutrition. Travis likely needed blood. The thought of Travis drinking blood from the supply he'd shown Cal stored in his refrigerator, made Cal's stomach turn. Not for the reason he thought it should, though. He wasn't sure why or when the feeling of Travis drinking bagged blood instead of having it fresh from him even became a thought in his mind.

A little over a month ago, he was horrified Travis had to drink blood, needed blood to survive. Now, he was almost as horrified he wanted to give Travis the nutrition he needed. Still, horrified at himself or not, the thought caused a spike of fear to increase his heart rate. However, if he were honest with himself, Cal wasn't sure if his fear was over what Travis would need to do in order to feed or how he'd react to Travis feeding from him. It was the thought he would enjoy feeding Travis that made his heart race almost uncontrollably.

"What is wrong?" Travis had to ask because Cal's sudden racing heart concerned him.

Travis didn't release his gentle embrace until Cal's paws, all four of them, pushed against his body. Cal didn't bolt away after he stood and for that Travis was grateful.

"Why don't you get a shower and I'll make you breakfast," Travis offered before he sat up then stood next to the bed. "I'll make you some French toast." Travis informed him and before Cal could make a single sound, he left the bedroom.

Chapter Fifteen

Travis stepped into his kitchen and retrieved the eggs from the refrigerator. He also pulled out a bag of his stored blood. He needed to feed and hoped Cal would take him up on his suggestion to shower, so he could do so. Telling the young garoul he needed blood to survive was vastly different than letting Cal see him drink his breakfast from a goblet.

Travis placed the bag of blood in his microwave and set it to warm up while he grabbed the bread from his counter and retrieved the cinnamon. He was so focused on getting the items he needed to make French toast, including a bowl and pan, he never detected the soft footfalls of Cal stepping into the kitchen.

Cal walked across the living room carpet and was surprised Travis didn't turn around to acknowledge him. If he was still in his feline form, he might not have been surprised Travis didn't even turn his way. But he wasn't. It was clear Travis was getting ready to prepare breakfast. It was also clear the microwave was humming and Cal could only think of one reason that would be the case.

The microwave beeped and Travis reached for a goblet from an overheard cabinet. If he was lucky enough, he could feed before Cal finished his shower and came out for breakfast. He had just opened his microwave door and pulled out his warmed bag of blood when Cal's voice scared the ever-living hell out of him.

"Do you prefer that?"

The curiosity in Cal's tone was clear and for a moment Travis was so stunned by the question that he forgot his meal which was warm in the palm of his hand.

Once more, Cal was surprised he'd caught Travis off guard. It was clear he had by the way the life drinker froze and didn't do anything, but hold the bag of blood. It wasn't his intention to make Travis feel uncomfortable or self-conscious for heating up the blood he needed to survive, but based on Travis' reaction he'd done just that.

"I thought you would shower," Travis commented and had to force himself to place his warmed-up blood on the counter.

"I didn't need a shower," Cal replied and waited for Travis to turn around and look at him.

The sexy bartender didn't. Instead, Travis kept his back to him and Cal didn't like that at all. He wanted to see Travis' steel grey eyes again, wanted to see the life drinker's level a gaze of compassion, caring, and want on him.

Now that Travis was aware of Cal's presence, he easily heard his approach. Travis wasn't ashamed of drinking blood. He'd been alive for way too long for that to be the case. Still, he wanted to shield Cal from this side of him. Apparently, Cal wasn't going to let him because he felt the man's arms snake around his waist and Cal pressed his body flush along Travis' back.

"You didn't answer me," Cal whispered against the nape of Travis' neck.

Cal had no idea where his boldness came from, but Travis had been so kind and made Cal feel things he'd never felt before. So, Cal wanted to give him something in return. Plus, he really wanted to feel Travis' mouth on his body.

"Cal," Travis breathed out in almost a warning.

He wasn't starving or injured to the point he had no control over his hunger, but Travis was sure Cal wasn't aware of how tempted he was to taste the small garoul. So, Travis braced his hands on his counter and tried to ignore how his body was reacting to Cal pressed against him.

"You're hungry," Cal whispered. "I'll feed you. I want to."

The boldness Cal had felt only moments before turned into insecurity when he offered to feed Travis. He had no idea what feeding the life drinker entailed exactly aside from what he'd seen on TV and in movies. Still, just the thought of Travis' mouth against his neck had him growing hard. He had no doubt Travis could feel his erection, but he really didn't care.

Travis inhaled so quickly when he heard Cal's words his intake of breath sounded like a hiss. He not only could feel Cal's arousal, but also smell it in the air around them. If Travis hadn't already been hard from feeling Cal's arms wrapped around his waist and the garoul pressing flush against his back, the scent of Cal's arousal would have made his dick feel like steel. In fact, it almost did already.

"I really would like to feed you, Travis," Cal whispered again before he placed another kiss on the nape of Travis' neck.

Travis barely suppressed the moan which threatened to escape his throat at the feel of Cal's warm lips against his skin. His fingers gripped the counter harshly in an effort to refrain from spinning around to touch Cal in return. Instead of doing just that, Travis' pushed his desire down and gave serious thought to whether he should feed from the sexy blonde who'd been practically consuming his thoughts every waking moment since they met. That said a lot considering he didn't sleep.

It was more than clear Cal was just as attracted to him as he was to the small garoul and it had nothing to do with the hard-on he felt pressing against his ass. Travis clearly had seen Cal's attraction to him in the man's Bahama blue eyes on several occasions and had no doubt Cal had seen the same reflected in his own.

Still, Travis was trepidatious over taking Cal up on his offer. He was concerned Cal was only offering to feed him because the small garoul felt he owed Travis something. Travis had to ensure that wasn't the case before he allowed himself to taste Cal in the most intimate way for his kind.

"You don't owe me anything, Cal. So, if that is why you are offering, I must decline."

Cal remained silent for several moments. His offer to feed Travis did have something to do with repaying the life drinker for his kindness. However, feeding Travis had more to do with wanting the man than anything else.

"You've been nothing but kind to me, Travis, but that is not why I am offering." Cal paused, but didn't move his lips away from the scant inches to Travis' neck. "I'm attracted to you, want more than just your kindness to help me, and I am tired of not doing anything about how I feel."

Travis had no choice but to release his death grip on the counter and spin around to face Cal. Had Travis not been very aware of their position before he turned, he likely would have head butted Cal. He didn't though. Instead, he gazed into Cal's beautiful blue eyes. All he saw was desire and want which couldn't be faked. Travis' hands rested on Cal's hips and his change in position caused Cal's hands to rest on his lower back. The moan he bit back before escaped his lips now when their jean-covered cocks lined up perfectly.

"Are you sure?" Travis forced himself to ask.

Cal wasn't surprised when Travis' concern for him made another appearance. However, it wasn't Travis' concern for his well-being Cal wanted at the moment. No, it was their mutual attraction to one another Cal wanted to explore and experience. So, Cal did the only thing he could think of to convince the sexy as sin bartender. He kissed the ever-living hell out of the man.

Travis barely had a moment to realize Cal's intent before the beautiful blonde's tongue was almost harshly seeking entrance into his mouth. Of course, Travis opened and he knew his first taste of Cal would forever be branded into his mind. That was more than fine with Travis as they fought for control of the kiss.

He was actually startled by Cal's aggressiveness. The small garoul had been so cautious of strangers, so skittish, Travis would have never expected Cal to be anything other than passive when it came to sex. To say Travis was happy this wasn't the case would have been an understatement.

They were both breathing hard through their noses when Travis pulled back only far enough to whisper against Cal's luscious lips. "Hold on," Travis told Cal even though the man still had his arms wrapped firmly around his waist.

Cal was grateful for the minimal warning Travis gave him with his request. Otherwise, he may have panicked when one moment they were in Travis' kitchen and the next he found himself flat on his back atop Travis' bed with the gorgeous man pressing him down into the mattress. Travis' life drinker speed was a blessing since Cal would rather be in the man's bed than ravishing him in the kitchen. Though at this point, Cal would ravish or be ravished wherever the hell Travis wanted.

Cal's moan was music to Travis' ears and when he felt Cal trying to remove his T-shirt, Travis pushed up slightly. The move caused his aching cock to press down against Cal's and forced him to break their kiss. Cal seemed to groan in disappointment from the loss of Travis' lips, but his hands never stopped in their mission to remove Travis' shirt.

All Cal could do was smile when he felt Travis brace his weight on first one then the other arm to allow Cal to free him of his sleeves. Cal used both hands to pull the T-shirt over Travis' head and paid no mind to where the cotton cloth landed when he tossed it away. Of course, Travis' mouth was back on his, so Cal didn't care where the damn thing landed. In fact, it wasn't even a thought since his mind was once more consumed with the taste of Travis.

Travis wanted, hell needed, to feel Cal's skin. Gently, he braced himself on one arm again and only lifted away enough so their chests no longer touched. He never broke their hungry kiss when he extended his nails into sharp points and hooked a finger in the collar of Cal's T-shirt. The cloth ripped like a knife slicing through soft butter and Travis finally made skin to skin contact when he lowered himself once more.

Another moan surrounded them and Cal wasn't sure if it was his, Travis' or them both echoing the sound at the same time. His need to feel all of Travis against his naked body and inside him was so great he didn't hesitate to move a hand off Travis' back to squeeze between them in order to get to their jeans. Thankfully, Travis lifted his hips again to grant him access even if Cal's dick protested the sudden lack of friction Travis provided by rutting down against him.

Getting them naked was taking too long as far as Travis was concerned. So, he forced himself to break away from Cal's delicious mouth and used his life drinker speed to get them both naked. His lips were back on Cal's before the beautiful man likely even noticed he'd moved.

Cal was suddenly naked. If he hadn't experienced how fast Travis could move, he'd have thought the sexy bartender had used magic to undress them. Another sensuous moan escaped Cal's lips into their kiss when he felt Travis' leaking dick slide against his throbbing hard-on. If he didn't get Travis in him *now,* he would provide them a lot more slick when he exploded his orgasm between them. As much as Cal didn't want to stop the incredible taste and feeling of Travis' tongue battling his, he forced himself to tilt his head back to break their all-consuming kiss.

Travis gave no thought to Cal moving his head back. No, he just continued to run his mouth along Cal's jaw and nip everywhere his lips touched. He didn't stop grinding down into Cal's body, either. Even though Cal tilting his head back exposed the pretty garoul's rapidly pulsating jugular.

"You have to fuck me," Cal somehow managed to pant out. "I want to feel you in me when I cum."

Travis pulled his lips away from Cal's smooth skin. He desperately wanted to be buried deep inside the small garoul, but he didn't just want to be some random hook-up where all they did was fuck and go their separate way or become friends with benefits. He wanted more than to just bust a nut with the gorgeous man who lay beneath him. He hadn't felt so strongly for someone in more years than he wanted to think about, but Cal's panted request made him think about how he really felt toward the small garoul. Travis lifted his head and met Cal's pupil blown gaze.

"I want to do more than just *fuck* you, Calvin," Travis whispered quietly. "I want to make love to you and make you mine. I want to be yours, too," Travis admitted and watched Cal's blue eyes grow wide. "If you just want to fuck, we can do that, but I'd really like this to be something more than just getting off."

Cal was speechless at Travis' declaration. He'd never had anyone want more from him than a quick release to satisfy a hunger which was due to attraction. He always believed no one would want him for something else. Travis saying he did, left him without words to reply. All he managed to do was give a dumbfounded nod while he stared up into Travis' storm grey eyes.

Travis was more than aware his words were not what Cal expected to hear. Cal's surprised reaction was enough to let Travis know the beautiful man had never been in a loving relationship. Travis wanted to be the first for this just like he'd been for Cal's first date. The man deserved to be loved and Travis could admit he'd already given his heart to the skittish garoul at some point over the last few months. He could only hope Cal gave him his heart in return. Still, he wasn't sure what Cal's nod was confirming.

"Will you let me make love to you, beautiful?"

The pressure which made Cal's chest ache was different than the fear he was used to feeling when the same tightness made an appearance. His racing heart was also different. It wasn't due to fear or arousal. No, it was due to something else entirely. What, he had no words to explain. The feeling scared him, although he was confident, he had nothing to fear from Travis. He had never been made love to before and the thought made him slightly nervous.

Is making love different than fucking? What if I am not good at it? Will I lose Travis? Would he want nothing to do with me anymore?

The questions wouldn't stop bombarding Cal's mind. The answers his mind provided caused tears to well in his eyes until they spilled over and gravity caused them to run down toward his ears in an effort to reach the bed beneath him.

Cal's reaction was not what Travis expected. The tears flooding from the stunning blue eyes which Travis easily became lost in and the feeling of the beautiful garoul's flagging erection caught Travis totally off guard. Both worried him and seeing Cal cry broke Travis' heart since he was sure his words were the cause.

"Don't cry, beautiful." Travis leaned on his elbows and gently used his fingers to wipe away the tears from Cal's cheeks to where they ended by his ears.

Cal sniffled and tried to stop his tears from falling. The mood was ruined and it was all his fault. Still, he couldn't have stopped his reaction to Travis' words and couldn't do anything about it now. All he could do was hope Travis would understand and still want him after this disaster. He was pretty sure the life drinker would if Travis' past behavior toward him was anything to go by, but even that thought couldn't stop the sudden fear he felt that this time could be different.

The plethora of emotions which swirled in Cal's crystal blue eyes weren't easy for Travis to read. They were there, though, and Travis was determined to know what they meant.

"Tell me what is wrong, beautiful, and how I can help," Travis requested quietly. "Please."

"I...I...," Cal sniffed and forced himself to just spit out what he was feeling. "I don't know how to make love. What if I am no good? What if I suck at it? I could fuck it up." Cal sniffed again before he pressed on. "What if I am not good enough? I don't want you to be disappointed or think you've wasted your time... you won't want anything to do with me then."

"Oh, Calvin." Travis dipped his head and placed a gentle, loving kiss on Cal's lips before he pushed Cal's curly blonde locks back from his forehead. He continued to run his fingers through the silky strands and he continued. "There is no right or wrong way to make love when it comes from your heart. I also have no doubt you are good enough for me. In fact, you will be the best lover I've ever had since I am pretty sure you feel toward me as I do you." Travis used his thumbs to wipe away a fresh trail of tears. "I could never be disappointed with you and you will *never* be a waste of my time." Travis gave Cal another soft kiss. "And the only way I wouldn't want anything to do with you is if that was what you wanted."

"I don't!" Cal said quickly and was rewarded with a smile from Travis which made his heart race and the feeling in his chest become stronger.

"Good, because it would break my heart if that was what you wanted." Travis was relieved to see a small smile spread Cal's lips. "Let me make love to you, beautiful?

Cal nodded even though he still had doubts about being able to make love to Travis in return. All he'd ever done was get off quickly in back rooms and alleys. He'd never even had sex in a bed, let alone with someone as caring and sexy as Travis. Still, he was willing to try and hoped the feelings which were so new and scary were those of love he had dreamed of feeling.

"Please," Cal barely managed to say before Travis' smile seemed to widen and his lips were on him again.

The frantic hunger they felt for each other was muted, but the want and desire hadn't disappeared at all due to their conversation. Instead, it seemed even greater when Cal felt Travis' lips upon his again. Cal opened to him and the kiss was almost too gentle for the craving he felt for the man. Travis wanted to make love to him, so Cal allowed the sexy man to set their pace regardless of how much he wanted Travis' aggressiveness to return.

Travis wanted to consume Cal as he had earlier, but after the small garoul bared his insecurities, he was hesitant to do so. He didn't want Cal to equate their love making to the quick fucks he was more than sure were Cal's only experience with sex. No, he wanted to make love to the beautiful man beneath him, so he kept his screaming need to possess the small garoul in check.

However, as much as he wanted to take things slower after their brief conversation, Travis' body had a mind of its own. He couldn't stop rutting against Cal's renewed erection or stop his hands from trying to feel as much of the pretty man's skin that was pressed along the length of his body. The return touches, the almost desperate touches, of Cal's hands running along his flanks only encouraged Travis to give into the hunger which was rapidly consuming them.

Chapter Sixteen

The more Cal touched Travis, the more the man started to aggressively touch him in return. Cal was initially concerned he would do something wrong when it came to making love to Travis. However, feeling the sexy life drinker's hips press down into him and Travis' cock glide against his aching erection caused Cal to forget every concern. Any worries he had about what he should do to make love fled his mind the more Travis touched him. He couldn't deny the hunger he felt for the man nor stop his body from conveying his want and need to feel more of Travis.

The soft kisses Travis initially gave him during their brief exchange of words soon disappeared and the battle of lips and tongues from prior to his words finding voice resumed. Cal moaned. He could do nothing else especially when Travis allowed him to suck on his tongue. Travis' matching groan of pleasure and hand tightening on his hip gave Cal greater confidence.

Travis understood Cal's seemingly passiveness after the small garoul confessed his insecurities. Travis was more than sure Cal was following his lead regardless of the man's desire to do otherwise. So, he was relieved Cal seemed to lose himself in their desire for one another once again. He had every intention to make love to Cal. He also had every intention to show the beautiful man making love didn't mean muting the desire and hunger they felt for each other.

So, not only did Travis encourage Cal to treat his tongue like a cock and suck away, but he couldn't resist forcefully grinding down against him. The warm wet sensation of their combined pre-cum as Travis provided them both the friction they sought when their cocks slid together was enough to make them both groan with pleasure.

It took almost no time for Cal's mind to abandon any thoughts of what making love to Travis might require of him. The feel of the life drinker's naked body pressing him down into the mattress and Travis' hard cock rubbing almost harshly against his along with the man's taste spurred him on. The desire and hunger Cal initially felt in the kitchen returned in full force and all Cal wanted was for Travis to fill him.

So, he didn't hesitate to move his hand between them. He didn't hesitate to wrap his hand around Travis' cock and nudge him enough to make Travis pull his hips back slightly. Travis never stopped kissing him before he moved Travis' cock down beneath his balls where one thrust would fill him the way he wanted to feel the gorgeous bartender atop him.

Travis was consumed by Cal's taste, by Cal's hands on his body, but not to the point he was oblivious to the small garoul's hand grasping his cock and requesting he lift his hips by touch alone. The feel of Cal's hand grasping him and the head of his sensitive, dripping, cock dragging over the underside of Cal's balls until it rested perfectly against Cal's entrance caused Travis to shiver and break their kiss. Cal tilting his head to expose his throbbing jugular once their lips parted was almost too much for Travis not to cum all over where he wanted to be buried.

Cal felt Travis shudder once he placed the life drinker where he desired to feel him to the fullest. He didn't give any thought of needing lube. He thought of nothing but the silky feel of the head of Travis' cock rubbing against his hole. Garouls healed quickly and he was too desperate to feel Travis inside him to give a shit about lube. Apparently, Travis wasn't.

"Need lube, beautiful," Travis breathed against Cal's lips before he moved.

Travis was back in place between Cal's legs and pressing the head of his cock where he was going to be buried before Cal could even reply. He had the capped popped on the Swiss Navy and his fingers were coated in a matter of seconds. Travis forced himself to slow down when he circled his lubed fingers around Cal's hole. He could already feel Cal's entrance twitching, so Travis didn't hesitate to push his finger into the hot heat he would soon feel wrapped around his painfully hard cock.

Cal let out a long drawn out moan of pure pleasure and pressed his hips down toward the bed to feel more of Travis' finger. It wasn't enough regardless of how flush Travis' hand was pressed against his ass.

"More," Cal breathlessly panted out.

Travis kissed and nipped along Cal's jaw. He purposely stayed away from Cal's neck. The desire to feed was strong, but his want to see Cal come undone from pure pleasure, pleasure he gave, was greater than his desire to feed. He was more than happy to fulfill Cal's request for more, so he inserted another finger. Scissoring them rewarded him with another long drawn out moan from Cal.

He couldn't help the smile which spread his lips against Cal's jaw from knowing he'd given Cal enough pleasure to cause the sound. It was a sound he wanted to hear once more and one that would be branded on his mind, like Cal's taste, even if he never heard it again. Travis swore to himself he would do whatever it took to hear that sound again.

"Travis," Cal panted out while he attempted to push his hips down further to feel more of Travis' fingers.

Travis hadn't done more than insert two fingers, but Cal really didn't need him to do more. In fact, if Travis moved his fingers with any purpose other than loosening him up, Cal was sure to explode between their sweaty abs which were still providing him delicious friction. Still, Cal needed more. He was so desperate to get the full feeling he sought, he felt no shame in begging for what he wanted.

"More. Please, Travis. More."

The desperation in Cal's almost ragged panting request made Travis' hard-on throb painfully and his want to bury his cock in the tight, hot, heat surrounding his fingers was almost too much. Somehow, he managed to add a third finger. He could feel every muscle surrounding his fingers quiver and his cock twitched in anticipation to be surrounded by the sensation. However, Travis never stopped kissing and nibbling along Cal's smooth jaw to distract himself while he prepared Cal because the taste of the small garoul was intoxicating.

Cal moved his hips again. Travis hadn't moved his fingers since he added a third. It still wasn't enough. Cal wanted, desperately needed, to feel more. Right. Fucking. Now. He vaguely felt Travis' mouth and teeth exploring his jaw. The sensation felt wonderful, but not nearly as incredible as the fingers in his ass he was trying to bury further by pressing down into Travis' palm.

"Travis," Cal managed to pant out in a whisper.

Travis didn't need Cal to again voice what he wanted. The beautiful blonde's tone and movement of his hips was more than enough to tell Travis not only what his lover needed, but that Cal thought he was prepped enough. He removed his three fingers even though he felt he hadn't prepared Cal nearly enough to take him. Cal groaned and Travis was sure the sound had everything to do with the sudden loss of fullness.

However, Cal's groan barely dissipated between their panting breaths before Travis thrust in. His moan from feeling the hot, tight heat suddenly gripping him was barely louder than Cal's sigh which sounded like one of pure relief. Cal's grasp on his sides grew tighter and didn't loosen until he was buried hilt deep.

Travis stilled to allow Cal to adjust to his length and girth and at the same time he stopped peppering Cal's jaw with kisses and nibbles. He lifted his head away from Cal's chin and met his lover's stunning blue eyes. Travis could easily become lost within the sea of blue which returned his gaze.

Cal sighed in relief. Pure fucking relief when he felt the burn and stretch of Travis totally filling him up. He'd had several men fuck him before, but Cal was more than sure none of them had been as endowed as Travis, Maybe that was why the life drinker felt so good filling him, but Cal doubted the size of Travis' long, thick dick had anything to do with the feeling causing pressure behind his sternum. None of the men he allowed to fuck him in alleys or back rooms in gay bars ever caused his chest to feel this tight. It was this feeling which made Cal believe Travis was really making love to him. Travis hadn't even moved yet and even though Cal was reveling in the sensation of being full, it wasn't enough to explain the other feelings that were bombarding him.

"You okay, beautiful?" Travis asked even though Cal's gaze never left his.

Cal didn't wince or push on his hips to indicate he should stop his desire to sink deep. His lust filled gaze never changed to one which indicated the sexy garoul was in pain, either. Still, Travis felt the need to ask and remain still for a few moments before he gave into his urge to move.

"I'm more than okay," Cal replied to assure Travis and he gave the man he wanted to spend all his time with a smile.

Cal pulled on his hips causing Travis to sink the scant millimeters deeper. Another moan escaped Travis' lips before he lowered his head and kissed Cal with a gentleness he was more than sure the small garoul wasn't used to. He was right when Cal didn't accept his gentle kiss, but instead aggressively attacked his mouth at the same time he shifted his hips again in a silent plea for Travis to move.

Travis' intentions to take things slow to show Cal love making could be just as enjoyable, if not more so, than just fucking evaporated. He pulled back and thrust forward harshly. The sound of pleasure, almost one of shock, from his action escaped Cal's lips. He wanted to hear it again, so he grasped Cal's hip tightly and repeated the movement.

Cal couldn't have stopped his shout of almost pure bliss into their kiss when Travis pulled back and thrust into him. The incredible pleasure from Travis' initial thrust was beyond anything he'd experienced during the quick fucks he'd had so far in his life. Cal wasn't naïve enough to think the mind-blowing pleasure he felt from just one of Travis' thrusts had anything to do with love.

However, the feelings Travis was currently causing him to experience, both emotionally and physically, made him wonder if he actually *was* in love with the man. Cal had no chance to consider the thought before Travis slammed into him again and tore another almost wounded animal noise from his throat.

Travis forced himself to push up from where he was bracing his weight on his forearms next to Cal's head. Cal's head was arched back, exposing his neck and tempting Travis, so he settled back on his heels and grasped Cal's hips to pull his pretty lover onto his cock with every thrust.

Travis had no desire to dilute the mind-blowing ecstasy they were both experiencing by pushing desire and want into his bite while feeding. He would still do so when he fed from Cal, but he wanted his beautiful garoul to experience everything Travis could give him without the delusion he normally would have created when he fed from a live meal.

Cal was making noise. Sounds which were either groans, moans, or something else entirely were echoing almost in tune with the slapping of bare skin. He was vaguely aware of the noises he was making; noises he'd never made while seeking relief in an ally or a dark back room in a gay bar. Of course, the insane feelings of almost explosive bliss which were currently causing him to vibrate under Travis were like nothing else he'd experienced before, either. He was so caught off guard when his orgasm exploded from the head of his cock he momentarily stopped breathing. A second later he made what was sure to be an inhuman noise when his back arched off the bed and his hands flailed for purchase on Travis' body before he took a deep panting inhale of breath.

Travis was so struck by the beauty of Cal's release his thrusts into the tight heat of the garoul shuddered. Seeing Cal's back arch while his cum exploded from his pretty cock, which hadn't even been touched, and hearing the sound Cal made which drowned out the slapping of skin ripped Travis' orgasm from him so fast that it was almost painful.

He wanted to keep his gaze on Cal to witness every second of his lover's orgasmic bliss, but his own release wouldn't allow him to do so. His hands tightened on Cal's hips at the same time his head fell back and his eyes had no choice but to close while every nerve in his body seemed to vibrate with pleasure. Travis was still panting hard when he finally managed to open his eyes and allowed his head to fall forward to look at Cal again.

Cal had seen more than stars when his dick exploded to decorate his abs and chest. He'd seen what heaven was surely. If heaven wasn't what he saw when he orgasmed then when he was finally able to focus on Travis, the man was. Seeing every muscle on Travis' body taut while his head was thrown back in what was clear ecstasy couldn't be described as anything other than seeing an angel from heaven. Just knowing he'd caused Travis' to look like a gorgeous fallen angel consumed with pleasure filled Cal's chest with that unidentified emotion again. He was still panting to catch his breath, but able to smile at Travis when the life drinker's steel grey eyes met his.

Cal's breath hitched at the intensity of Travis' gaze. He wished he was better at reading emotions just by looking someone in the eye. He wasn't, but didn't fear the look Travis leveled on him now. So, he smiled again at the man who made him have strange feelings.

Cal's smile, hitch of breath, and spread of lips was too much for Travis to resist kissing. He leaned forward and did just that. His movement caused a low grown to escape Cal's lips and he kissed his garoul lover again. Another moan from Cal vibrated against Travis' lips while his tongue tasted the pretty blonde who he knew now owned his heart.

"I planned on making slow love to you," Travis informed after he pulled back and met Cal's stunning blue eyes. "Instead, you pulled the love right out of me fast and hard." Travis sat back on his heels, but not back far enough to slip free of the warmth which still encased his semi-hard dick.

Cal smiled almost shyly. He'd never heard anyone apologize over how sex had gotten them off. It was weird, but weird in a good way which flooded him with a new kind of warmth and made his chest tighten again.

"Is that a bad thing?' Cal dared to ask even though he was pretty sure it wasn't.

"Not at all." Travis grinned.

"Good." Cal nodded and let another genuine smile spread his lips. They smiled at each other for a moment before Cal spoke again. "You're still hungry," Cal stated with surety before he tilted his head and bared his neck. His desire to give Travis what he needed hadn't lessened even after the incredible sex they'd just shared. If anything, the urge to provide Travis the substance he needed to survive was even stronger.

Travis watched Cal tilt his head and stared at his pulsing jugular. His cock that had been slowly deflating in the warm heat of Cal's ass now twitched. It wasn't a sexual reaction per se, just a reaction to feeding from a person as opposed to getting the nutrition he needed from a bag.

"Are you sure, beautiful?" Travis repeated the question he'd asked the small beautiful garoul earlier.

"I was sure before," Cal responded. "I want to do this. Not just because it is something you need and I am sure it's better than the bagged stuff you usually use, but because I want to give you what you need. I have feelings for you that I don't even know how to describe. And... I want to feel your mouth on me, against my neck, in my neck, and know I am taking care of you as much as you've taken care of me."

"Offering your neck is not necessary..." Travis began, but Cal cut him off.

"I know," Cal countered and struggled to find the words he needed to explain why he wanted to give this part of himself to Travis. "I want to do this, Travis. For you. For me. For us."

Cal wasn't sure his explanation was enough or even coherent enough for Travis to grasp what he meant and why he desired to feed him.

For us.

Cal's mention that he considered them an 'us' was enough to erase Travis' concerns and trepidations over why the beautiful man was offering his neck. The fact Cal was considering them a couple filled Travis with joy and made Travis' heart soar.

"Okay," Travis whispered and cupped Cal's cheek before he moved Cal's head back into an angle to kiss him.

Cal sank into the softness of Travis' lips. He enjoyed, hell delighted, in Travis' taste and didn't protest when his sexy bartender's lips left his mouth and once more kissed along his jaw. Travis was still firmly seated in his ass and Cal's could feel him hardening. Cal's own dick was springing back to life and he couldn't help but shift his hips to feel more of Travis. The urge to gain friction against Travis' abs was undeniable. He was so focused on the fullness which was increasing in his ass and the friction he sought for his throbbing cock, he never even felt Travis' fangs sink deep into his jugular.

Chapter Seventeen

The first burst of flavor from Cal's blood exploded on Travis' taste buds and made him groan at the same time he swore fireworks exploded behind his closed eyes. It had been sometime since Travis had had a fresh meal, but he was well aware Cal's indescribable taste had nothing to do with how long it had been since he'd fed from someone. Feeding from garouls always tasted better than feeding from humans, but the deliciousness which was pure Cal tasted like nothing he'd ever experienced before in his long lifetime.

Travis' ear was so close to Cal's pretty pink lips which were fast becoming Travis' second favorite flavor to taste that his moan of pleasure sounded loud. Just hearing Cal's enjoyment from his bite was enough to ensure Travis didn't need to push pleasure into his feeding. He was tempted to do so anyway, but when Cal canted his hips causing him to sink just that much deeper into Cal's tight heat all thoughts of needing to provide simulated pleasure fled Travis' mind.

Cal couldn't explain the sensation of Travis feeding from his neck just like he couldn't explain the foreign feeling in his chest. He felt joy and happiness for being able to give Travis what he needed, but the other feeling was larger, more intense, and he wished he had a word to identify it. Maybe that word was love.

However, whatever the word might be it didn't really matter while he reveled in the sensation of Travis feeding and filling him up again. Cal unconsciously moved his hips to feel more of Travis' hardness buried deep within him. Another moan escaped his lips and he never noticed he used his shoulders to lift his head and bring his neck closer to Travis' mouth.

Another deep throated groan escaped around Travis' lips as he suckled on Cal's throat. He almost lost himself in the sounds Cal made and the clenching of Cal's ass around his throbbing cock. Almost. He didn't though and instead forced himself to seal the wounds he'd inflicted on the pale creamy skin of Cal's neck. Travis didn't lift his head up right away, but he did push his hips down.

Cal wasn't so lost in ecstasy to not feel when Travis stopped feeding and began to move his hips in small grinding circles. Still, as good as Travis felt hitting his prostate it didn't distract from the loss Cal felt when Travis stopped feeding. He wanted to feel Travis' fangs back in his neck and feel Travis' gentle sucks pulling the blood Travis needed from his body. Cal was about to voice his request when Travis pulled his hips back just enough to thrust again and pull a cry from his throat.

Travis adjusted his arms from being braced next to Cal's head to under his lover's so he could grasp Cal's shoulders. With every thrust, he used his hands to pull Cal's body down toward his hips. He felt Cal's hands grasping his hips and mirror him by pulling Travis closer. Cal's hard cock rubbed against his abs and Cal's previous release only made the slide against his skin feel so damn good that Travis had no desire to change their position.

Cal felt like he couldn't breathe. His panting breath and Travis' weight had nothing to do with it, either. No, it was the intense feeling in his chest combined with the spine-tingling buildup of his orgasm which was making him lightheaded. His sharp cry caused from his orgasm once again soaking into their pressed together stomachs only seem to spur Travis on. Three more harsh thrusts and Travis grasped his shoulders almost painfully before he seemed to sink into him further, if that were even possible, before he stilled and Cal felt heat fill him inside.

Travis was breathing too hard for any sound to escape his throat before or after he exploded his release into Cal. All he managed to do was rest his sweaty forehead on the bed and attempt to catch his breath. He could feel Cal trying to do the same. The warm air of Cal's breath caressing his shoulder made Travis shiver which resulted in another moan from Cal.

Cal didn't seem to be in any hurry for him to roll off him and that was just fine with Travis. However, Travis soon noticed Cal's breaths become slow and steady, heard only in the way of sleep. He smiled to himself when he lifted his head and looked down to find Cal sound asleep.

His pretty garoul appeared not only resting peacefully, but much younger. Sweat soaked his blonde locks and Travis was careful not to wake his lover when he moved one arm from beneath Cal's shoulder so he could brush the damp strands off Cal's forehead. Cal only moved his head slightly as if into Travis' gentle touch. That small movement made Travis' heart swell again.

As he gazed down at the beautiful garoul, Travis could admit what he was currently feeling for the man could only be love. The thought didn't scare or bother him as much as he thought it would if he ever fell in love. Perhaps, he was calm and accepting of what he felt for

Cal because he was sure Cal felt the same if what he read in the man's beautiful blue eyes was any indication.

Travis was still smiling at his revelation when he slowly moved away from his lover. He didn't bother to clean Cal up before he pulled the comforter up to cover him. Travis liked the thought of Cal carrying his scent so everyone would understand he was taken. Plus, Cal could shower when he woke and the sheets could be washed.

Travis' smile never left his lips just like his gaze never left Cal's until he stepped into the bathroom to shower.

Cal lay on his side. His back arched when his arms and legs stretched out in front of him as if he were in his feline form. He didn't open his eyes until his stretch was complete. It was then the smell of breakfast being made reached him.

It didn't escape his notice he was still covered in his cum. Not all of it was dry, but what was caused his skin to itch. The dampness from what Cal was more than sure was their cum soaked into the comforter was enough to let him know he hadn't slept for long.

So, Cal crawled out from under the comforter and headed into the bathroom for a quick shower. Travis was waiting for him, a plate of French toast in his hand, when he stepped back into the bedroom. Cal didn't stop to get dressed. His nudity didn't bother him in the least and if the look in Travis' gaze was anything to go by, the life drinker wasn't bothered at all, either.

"Breakfast." Travis smiled and told his dick to behave since seeing Cal standing before him naked made him want to taste the beautiful garoul all over again.

Cal returned Travis' smile. "Smells delicious."

Cal took the few steps to the king-sized bed and pulled the comforter up to cover the mess they'd made. He promptly sat cross legged on the bed facing Travis.

"Are you going to eat with me or have you had enough to sate your hunger?" Cal was aware Travis ate normal food, but he didn't know if the sexy man who just handed him breakfast was still hungry or not.

Travis forced down a moan. His hunger for Cal would never be fully sated, he was sure, and it had nothing to do with the intoxicating taste of the man's blood. He dared to say as much.

"My hunger for you will never be sated, but my French toast is in the kitchen." Travis returned Cal's wide smile his words caused to spread Cal's plump lips. "Would you like some coffee?"

"Coffee would be great."

"Okay. I'll be right back."

Cal waited for Travis to return and get comfortable on the bed with him before he started to eat. Their conversation was light and comfortable. It was likely because Travis did all of the sharing about himself and never pressured Cal to do the same.

It was a few hours later when Cal noticed how late in the day it was. He really didn't want to leave, but he needed clean clothes if he was going to spend time at The Witch's Brew again while Travis worked. So, as much as he didn't want to leave, he had to.

"I need to get going," Cal began and could sense his words made Travis unhappy. "I don't want to go, but

I need fresh clothes before I see you later tonight." Those words returned the smile to Travis' lips that Cal was quickly becoming addicted to seeing.

"Okay." Travis stood and collected their breakfast dishes from where they placed them on the side of the bed. "I'll let you get dressed and call an Uber."

Travis bent and gave Cal a light kiss before he left his bedroom. He hated that Cal was going to leave because he wanted the man to stay so badly. Cal just looked so right sitting naked in the center of his bed, but he understood the small garoul's need to leave and didn't feel like the man was trying to escape him.

He still had no idea where Cal lived and could admit that bothered him more than just a little bit since he was aware Cal was hiding from Hunters. Still, Travis wouldn't pressure Cal for the information. He didn't want his beautiful garoul to feel threatened if keeping where he was staying secret made him feel safe. Travis trusted Cal to tell him when he was ready.

Cal couldn't help but smile again when Travis looked over his shoulder and shot him a wink before he closed the dishwasher. The man's sexy-as-sin winks were becoming just as addicting as his smiles. Cal stepped into the kitchen and didn't hesitate to close the distance between them. Travis' arms wrapped around his waist and the feeling of safety this man gave him was almost overwhelming. It caused the tightness he was sure was what love felt like to bloom in his chest again.

"My ride will be here in five minutes," Cal informed regretfully.

"I wish you'd never leave."

The words escape Travis' lips totally unbidden and he mentally cursed. However, the reaction he expected Cal to have, one of skittishness or panic as a result of feeling trapped, never made an appearance.

Travis' comment made the sensation in Cal's chest soar. He couldn't even find the words to express what it meant to him, made him feel, that Travis felt that way toward him. The feeling of being wanted to that extent was just too great, so Cal did the only thing he could think of: he kissed the hell out of the man who held him so securely in the safety of his embrace.

Travis couldn't be more pleased at Cal's reaction to his unintentional admittance of how he felt. If he had any doubt Cal had the same feelings for him as he did for his beautiful garoul they were now gone. The love and passion in Cal's kiss said everything the man didn't put to voice.

They were both aroused again from their kiss, but the irresistible hunger they felt from one another earlier didn't make an appearance. In fact, this kiss was slow and languid just like Travis intended their lovemaking to be when he had his stunning garoul beneath him in his bed. Unfortunately, and way too soon, the sound of Cal's cell phone vibrating from his back pocket caused them to break apart.

"That's my ride," Cal said and was sure Travis would hear his disappointment that his Uber had arrived so quickly.

"I know." Travis forced himself to gently push Cal away and out of his embrace. "I'll see you tonight, though?"

"You will." Cal leaned in and placed a quick kiss on Travis' lips before he made himself turn away and head for the door.

"I can't wait," Travis called out before Cal could disappear through his front door.

"Me either." Cal gave Travis another smile before he closed the door behind him.

Travis couldn't help but glare at the clock repeatedly while he worked. Time seemed to crawl by and the later it became, the more concerned he became for Cal's safety. There were no doubts his coworkers noticed, either. However, the club was too busy for them to actually have time to say anything. Though, their looks made it clear they perceived his change in behavior.

It was almost midnight and between glancing at the clock, serving customers, filling waitress orders, and looking toward the front door, Travis was on edge the longer Cal didn't appear.

He was more than sure what happened between them wasn't the cause for Cal's absence at his usual spot at the bar. That was what fueled Travis' worry for his beautiful garoul.

Cal hadn't expected his move to a different crappy motel to take so long, but between calling Ubers to take him to a new shithole and said shitholes not having any rooms which required him to call another Uber, he was running more than late for the time he planned to be at The Witch's Brew.

He only hoped Travis didn't think it had anything to do with him not wanting to see the sexy life drinker again. All he wanted to do was see Travis again and if he weren't so worried his father might find him, he wouldn't have changed crappy motels at all and would have been at The Witch's Brew hours ago.

He was here now, though. The large security doorman who Cal knew was a bear garoul after spending so much time talking with Travis that afternoon, gave him a smile when he got out of his Uber ride to the club. George was his name and seemed just as friendly as the previous times Cal came to the club. The man never spoke to him, but that wasn't the case tonight.

"You've had Travis worried, Cal."

Cal was momentarily taken aback. Not only by George telling him Travis was worried he hadn't arrived earlier, but also because the large garoul knew his name. The only way George would know his name was if Travis had spoken to his coworkers about him. Just that thought brought a smile to his lips.

"Just running late tonight. Had a few things to take care of," Cal replied as he stepped toward the open door of the club.

George gave him a nod and smile in return. "Well, I'm sure Travis will be happy you are here now. Have a good time."

"I'm sure I will," Cal said before he entered The Witch's Brew.

Travis' eyes locked onto his the second Cal cleared the doorway into the club. He wasn't sure if George gave his sexy man the heads up he'd finally arrived or whether or not Travis had been watching the door periodically for him. Or, maybe, Travis just sensed his presence because the life drinker fed from him. Cal thought that was possible even if he didn't know for sure. None of those options mattered to Cal, though, when their gazes connected across the crowded club. Nope. All that mattered to Cal as he walked toward the spot he usually occupied at Travis' bar was the almost blinding smile the man leveled on him.

Travis was so relieved and happy to finally see Cal he was sure not only did his coworkers notice the change in his body language, but some of his customers did as well since they followed his gaze. He quickly grabbed a bottle of water from the cooler and walked down the length of his bar toward his lover.

"Hey, beautiful," Travis greeted and placed the water in front of Cal. "I'm happy you came in."

Cal smiled at Travis. He sensed a rare hesitation or maybe it was a tinge of insecurity when Travis finished his greeting. Cal didn't like making Travis feel either if his being late was the cause of Travis' tone.

"I wouldn't be anywhere else." Cal assured. "Sorry I'm late, though."

"I was starting to worry that maybe," Travis trailed off. "It doesn't matter now that you are here."

Cal ignored whatever Travis was about to say when he mentioned the word worry. "How's your night been so far? You look busy."

Travis glanced over his shoulder. He was indeed busy. Several new customers were standing at the bar wanting drinks. Travis didn't want to care, but he did have a job to do.

"Yeah. I guess I need to go take care of them," Travis replied with a grin when he turned back to Cal.

"I'll be here," Cal assured Travis with another smile.

"I'll be back in a bit." Travis gave his lover a wink before turning back to work.

It was almost an hour before Travis was able to get back to Cal. Of course, not being close to his beautiful bobtail didn't stop him from constantly looking in Cal's direction. Cal's gaze was glued to him and every time Travis glanced at him another wide smile spread Cal's plump lips.

Cal could have been sitting alone in the bar while he watched Travis work with as much attention as he paid to anything else. The feeling of safety Travis gave him grew each time his sexy bartender looked his way to check on him. Cal hoped Travis would ask him to go home with him again. He wanted to be the one to ask, but couldn't work up the nerve. Cal was still trying to get over his nervousness to ask when Travis started walking back toward him with another bottle of water.

"How are you doing, pretty?" Travis gave Cal another wink before he placed the unopened water on the bar top.

Cal would've smiled wider if he could. "Watching you? Good."

Where his boldness came from Cal wasn't sure. However, he was grateful for it when Travis chuckled. Cal loved any sound Travis made, but his chuckles and outright laughs were his favorite. Well, aside from how Travis said 'pretty' and 'beautiful'.

"I want you to come home with me again tonight," Travis declared unabashedly.

If Travis hadn't already told him about the abilities life drinkers possessed, he would've thought the man read his mind. That wasn't one of Travis' abilities, though, so that could only mean Travis had to feel the same way toward him as he did the gorgeous life drinker.

The tightness in his chest which Cal decided could only be love bloomed again.

"I want that, too." Cal hesitated before he finished though. "I'd like to go get a change of clothes. If that's all right?"

Cal bringing anything to his house was more than all right as far as Travis was concerned. Actually, he wished his beautiful bobtail would bring everything he owned. The desire to ask Cal to just move in with him was strong, but Travis resisted the urge. He was concerned his skittish lover would feel trapped if he moved in since Travis was pretty sure Cal moved frequently to stay hidden from Hunters. So, for now, Travis would settle for every time Cal agreed to spend the night.

"That sounds good," Travis replied and glanced over his shoulder to check the time. 1:15. There was plenty of time for Cal to grab whatever he needed and return before closing.

Cal leaned sideways to see around Travis to view the bar clock. "Twenty-five minutes, tops, once my Uber picks me up." Cal grinned.

That wasn't as long as Travis had expected Cal to be gone and to say he was not only relieved, but happy, would've been an understatement. Travis leaned forward over his bar top and smiled when Cal matched his movement. He placed a kiss that was way too chaste on his lover's lips and was warmed when Cal groaned with disappointment when he pulled back.

"Hurry back," Travis whispered against Cal's lips before he gave his lover another quick peck and stepped back.

"See you soon," Cal promised and stood from his bar stool.

He only glanced back once before he was swallowed up by the crowd between Travis' bar and the front door of the club. Travis' gaze tracking his progress made his heart feel too large for his chest. It was a sensation he was coming to relish and couldn't wait to feel more of.

Chapter Eighteen

"Leaving already?" George asked the moment Cal stepped out of the club's front door.

Cal glanced at the large bear garoul and the man wasn't fast enough to erase the frown which graced his features. He gave George a smile. Of all the garouls who worked at The Witch's Brew which Cal was forcing himself to become comfortable around, George was the easiest, even if Cal could detect the faint trace of a predator from the man. Cal was aware bears were omnivores and it was likely the fact the man wasn't 100% carnivore which made him feel the way he did toward The Witch's Brew doorman.

"I'll be back," Cal replied. "I'm just going to grab some clothes."

Cal's comment brought a smile to George's lips. He returned it before he stepped away and pulled his cell phone from his back pocket. Cal leaned against the club's wall and punched in his request for a ride in his Uber app. He could feel the bass from the club's music coming through the wall and the thought of feeling it through his bar stool while he watched Travis work made him inpatient for his ride to arrive. Cal glanced at his Uber app and was already walking away from the wall when his app showed him his ride had pulled into the parking lot.

However, he was still looking at the app, specifically at the driver's photo and name, when he stopped next to the passenger door. The window was lowered and Cal bent down to look inside the car to verify it was actually *his* Uber. All of his breath left his chest and he froze as still as a statue after he looked up from his phone and met the driver's eyes.

No. No. No! Cal's mind screamed.

"Get in the fucking car, *son*." His father ordered and the gun he held didn't waver.

Run. Run. Get away, Cal's mind yelled at him, but his bobtail did what he always had when eye to eye with a predator. He froze. If he didn't move, the predator might not see him and move on. However, his calico side didn't stop his human side from reacting. He dropped his cell phone.

Three things happened at the same time: George called out to him, "you okay, Cal?" The gun fired, and Cal's bobtail broke out of his frozen state and he shifted.

Cal didn't even hear the gunshot, or George yell his name, or the car tires squeal out of the parking lot. In fact, his human side didn't even have any control over his garoul. He bolted. He fled. Ran full out toward The Witch's Brew's, thankfully, open door.

Unconsciously, he dodged and weaved through the club goers' legs until he reached the corner of Travis' bar he had claimed as his. Cal leapt. His front paws didn't even connect with the barstool before his back legs pushed off and propelled him over the bar top. How long he was airborne didn't even register before he landed on the black mats which covered the floor behind the bar. His bobtail took in his potential hiding places before any of them even became a conscious thought in Cal's human mind.

He was moving. Still running full out toward the other end of the bar were a cooler was abutted close to the bar sink. Cal didn't stop running until he scrambled under the sink and behind the bar cooler. He continued to squeeze himself into the tight space behind the cooler until he couldn't see a shred of light from the club.

Cal panted harshly through his mouth to catch his breath. His heart was beating so rapidly he thought it would explode from his chest and his legs still twitched to run in order to find a better place to hide. Cal's human side was well aware of everything he felt even though he was terrified to the point his bobtail had taken control.

We are fine. Nothing can reach us here, Cal tried to convince himself and focused on hearing if he was lying to himself.

All he heard were the normal sounds of the club. Well, mostly. As he focused, Travis' panicked voice reached his ears. Cal couldn't hear what his lover was saying, but his tone was obvious even under the blaring music of the club. He wanted to erase that tone, to let Travis know he was safe. Hell, he wanted to go to Travis and feel the safety he always did when around the man or in his arms. He couldn't, though. His bobtail wouldn't let him and Cal could admit at the moment, he really didn't want to move from the darkness in which he currently hid.

Travis had just set down two shots of Leg Spreaders when he caught a blur of movement at the end of his bar. His subconscious registered white, orange, and gray before his conscious mind recognized the blur as the outline of his bobtail lover clearing the end of his bar in a long leap.

By the time Travis turned to locate his lover's fleeing form, all he caught sight of was the nub of Cal's tail before he disappeared behind one of the bar coolers. Immediately, his head swiveled toward the end of his bar in search of whom or what scared his lover enough to risk shifting and running through a club full of humans.

Travis saw nothing but a few humans who looked startled or confused. He was sure they witnessed what they thought was a stray or house cat bolting through a nightclub. He should care about how the norms might react, but he didn't. All he cared about was what had sent his lover into a fear-laced flight to hide.

Travis pushed his earpiece. "George, what is going on? Talk to me!"

Cal had left the club, so if anyone knew what the hell was going on it would be George. A moment of silence filled Travis' ear as he stared toward the front door of the club and waited for George to reply. Travis was about to demand their bear garoul head of security respond when his ear filled with chatter.

"It had to be a Hunter," George said and Travis' blood ran cold.

"Did you get a good look at them?" Adam sounded pissed off.

"No." Travis could hear George beating himself up in the man's tone. "I thought it was just another Uber pulling up."

"Get the tag?" Adam's graveled voice reached Travis' ear.

"Yeah, likely won't get us anywhere, though. I should've paid more attention to what he looked like instead."

"The fucker fired a gun. The fact you got the plate is impressive enough," Adam said and Travis knew his boss' lover was trying to lessen George's guilt over what just went down.

However, hearing his lover had almost been shot sent a whole new level of ice racing through Travis' veins. He didn't think he'd seen any blood on Cal when his lover bolted behind the bar cooler, but then again Travis had only caught a glimpse of Cal when his lover scrambled to find a safe place to hide.

Travis' heart rate spiked further, if that were even possible, at the thought Cal could be injured in any way. The need to ensure Cal wasn't hurt was so strong Travis found himself on his knees, head under the bar sink, and trying to spot Cal behind the bar cooler.

He couldn't see shit. Even with his enhanced vision, all Travis saw was darkness. Not a glimpse of white fur or even Cal's bobtail shape. Travis had no doubt Cal was huddled down behind his bar cooler and the wall since he caught Cal's rear end scurrying between the bar wall and cooler.

"Cal?" Travis called out. He was sure his lover would hear him even though the club music volume hadn't changed. "Cal?"

Travis himself repeated and willed his lover to respond. Cal didn't. Travis didn't even get a lowly meow let alone a warning hiss which a typical feline garoul's response to feeling threatened. The lack of response from his lover only ratcheted up Travis' panic that Cal was actually shot.

He couldn't see Cal and even if he could, Travis was more than sure his lover was out of reach to touch. Not that he would attempt to grab his beautiful bobtail. But, if he could touch Cal to offer comfort, he would.

A hand on his back startled Travis to the point he almost banged his head on the sink above him. However, the near miss didn't stop him from glaring over his shoulder at the owner of the hand.

"Let him be." Travis continued to glare at Cat. It didn't matter to him that she could likely relate to what his lover was feeling since she was also a feline garoul.

His connection to Cal since he fed from his lover was so strong it was almost overwhelming. The panic and fear he felt made him want to do nothing other than make it go away. Surprisingly, it was realizing he only felt those emotions from Cal and not those of pain which would indicate injury that caused Travis' heart settle some.

"He will come out, Travis, when he's ready. When he feels the threat has passed, he'll come out. Right now, he needs the safety back there is giving him."

Travis stared at Cat for a few moments before he forced himself to crawl from beneath the sink and stand. Cat enveloping him in a tight hug caught Travis off guard enough he almost stumbled.

"He'll be okay. We'll make sure of it, but we need to get this place closed for the night first," Cat whispered against his throat because she was too short for her words to caress his ear.

Travis heard them just the same. He believed them, too, since he'd known Cat longer than any other garoul in his long lifetime. However, all Travis could do was nod against the top of her platinum blonde head to acknowledge he'd heard her words of reassurance. Cat let him go and exited the bar through the waitress area. It was while watching her walk away that Travis became aware there were still voices coming from his earbud.

"BT, do last call. We're closing early," Mikael informed all of his employees and Travis couldn't help but feel grateful his friend and boss was willing to close the club slightly early because of what happened concerning his lover.

Travis wasn't surprised, though, since Mikael made the safety of his family a priority above all else. Cal was family, too. He doubted his beautiful calico bobtail was even aware he'd been adopted into Mikael's family. Whether Cal was aware of his new family or not didn't matter. Just like it didn't matter Mikael would have more than likely adopted Cal regardless of Travis being in love with the man or not. Mikal had taken a liking to the bobtail and Cal now owning Travis' heart was probably just a bonus as far as his longtime friend and boss was concerned.

"Last call, y'all," BT announced. "I know, I know," BT continued. "It's earlier than normal, but you'll understand when you come back in next weekend."

Travis had no clue what BT was hinting at and really didn't give a shit. His mind was too absorbed with his lover still hiding behind his bar cooler to care. Still, he forced himself to fill the last drink orders of the night. He was working by rote and didn't care if he came off as rude while he served those last few drinks.

Cal remained hyper aware of what was going on in the club. Everything was slightly muted in his hiding place, but he easily heard when the DJ made last call. The sudden cut off of the club music was almost deafening and it took him a moment to adjust to the lack of thumping bass. Once he had, the sounds of the norms finishing their drinks and shuffling out of the club's front door filled his ears. Cal's panic laced fears seemed to reduce at the same rate the norms noises diminished.

The almost silence which filled the club, broken only by the sounds Cal knew were the closing activities of the Brew's employees helped him to relax more. The thought his father could still be waiting outside of the club never disappeared from his mind, but also knowing The Witches Brew employees were going about their regular routine mitigated some of his fear which threatened to take root in his chest again.

"Cal?"

Travis' soft, concerned, and caring voice broke over the background sounds of tables being cleared and glasses being washed. Cal instinctively purred and lifted his body up as much as the tight space he'd wedged himself in would allow.

"The club is empty aside from our family. It's safe to come out now," Travis informed him. It didn't escape Cal's notice that Travis referred to his coworkers as *their* family. "Please come out," Travis implored.

There was no way Cal could have resisted Travis' plea. Not that he wanted to, anyway. So, he began the tricky maneuvering which would allow him to crawl backwards out of his tight hiding space. Gaining his freedom from the tight confines between the cooler and bar top wall was more difficult than Cal expected.

He had no idea, or recollection, how he had wedged himself in so far behind the cooler. Every step backward he took was tricky due to the hoses and wires. Still, he placed paw after paw to inch his way back toward the end of the cooler which had been his safety.

Travis didn't hear a sound from behind his bar cooler. The appliance issued a low hum, but he strained to hear any movement from behind it to indicate Cal was coming out. It wasn't until he saw the nub of Cal's tail and his lover's white and gray striped rear legs that Travis actually released the breath he hadn't even realized he held.

His hands itched to reach out and scoop Cal up the moment the back half of his lover appeared from behind the stainless-steel cooler. Travis resisted, though, because the last thing he wanted to do was startle his skittish lover. So instead, he rested his hands on his thighs and waited for Cal to fully extract himself from where he'd been hiding behind the cooler.

"There you are," Travis whispered once Cal was fully exposed.

Cal purred. Those were the same words Travis said to him the first time he revealed himself to the man. They filled Cal with so much warmth that all he could do was purr and climb into his lover's lap. Travis' hands caressing down his flanks from his neck to tail gave Cal the impression the life drinker was not only showing him affection, but checking for injuries. Cal wasn't hurt, but had no way to assure his lover he was fine physically aside from purring his pleasure over being touched. So, he did. Not only purred, but pressed his body firmly against Travis' hard abs to feel more.

Travis was so relieved to feel Cal beneath his palms and pressing his silky fur covered body against him that he didn't want to move. However, enjoying how his lover made him feel while he sat on the filthy bar mat covered floor was not where he wanted them to stay.

"I'm going to take you home, now," Travis informed before he wrapped a hand under Cal's belly and stood.

Cal meowed and pushed his head under Travis' chin. His lover's reaction was all the permission Travis needed to carry Cal from behind the bar to the shadowed space beneath the club's stairs. Within a blink of an eye they stood in Travis' dark bathroom. Seconds later Travis lay on his bed. He still held Cal against his chest and continued to pet him from nape to tail nub.

Once Cal was held by Travis, he relaxed. Travis taking them to his house didn't even register before Cal realized he was kneading his paws and purring contently on Travis' chest while they lay on Travis' bed. However, as good as Travis' hands felt petting him; he wanted nothing more than to feel his sexy bartender's hands caressing his skin. So, he shifted.

Travis grunted. More in surprise than feeling the change in weight and size of his lover shifting forms atop him. "There you are," Travis whispered again.

"Here I am," Cal managed before he closed the distance between their lips.

Travis responded to Cal instantly. He had planned to ask Cal what had happened earlier, but all thought of inquiring about the night's events fled his mind at the first taste of his lover. It was more than clear Cal had other things on his mind, as well.

A groan escaped Travis' throat into their kiss when he felt Cal's hands not only under his T-shirt against his bare skin, but purposely pushing his shirt up with the intention of relieving him of the garment. Reluctantly, Travis let his hands fall away from Cal's sides and lifted his arms for Cal to strip him of the cotton.

Their mouths collided again and Travis once more reveled in his beautiful bobtail's taste. Still, he wasn't distracted enough by Cal's tongue exploring every bit of his mouth to not want to feel his lover's skin against him. Travis hooked his middle finger in the collar of Cal's shirt at the nape of his neck. With a thought, he extended his nail into a claw and sliced cleanly down the back of Cal's shirt. The material fell away to the sides of Cal's body and covered Travis' arms, but he didn't feel it at all. No, he felt Cal wiggling a hand between them to get to his jeans.

Cal needed to feel as much of Travis' bare skin as he could. He *needed* and mentally cursed what felt like a fumbling attempt to get the man he loved naked. Thankfully, Travis apparently felt the same because one second he was reaching between them and the next he found himself on his back.

Cal had no idea when Travis' mouth left his or when his life drinker managed to get him naked. Nope. No idea at all, but he didn't have a single brain cell to work it out because Travis' mouth was fully engulfing his hard shaft. The hot wet heat of Travis' mouth sucking him down sapped any control he had away and he thrust up.

If Travis thought, which he didn't, to be grateful for a single one of his species abilities it would have been his speed. Getting Cal naked barely took the time it would to blink. But of course, the time it took to get Cal naked enough to taste his pretty dick was the furthest thing from Travis' mind as he reveled in the taste of every drop of pre-cum which coated his tongue. He wanted to taste more so he sucked harder.

Cal pushed against Travis' shoulder. How he had the sense to do even that while Travis attempted to suck his brain out of the head of his dick, he had no clue. Still, he did.

"Gonna… Gonna cum," Cal sputtered.

Cal's warning issued on an almost strangled panting breath only spurred Travis on. He wanted to taste his beautiful garoul. Needed to feel his lover explode down his throat. He had every intention to make that happen, too.

Cal tensed. The tingling in his spine shot to his head and toes at the same time. His back arched and his toes curled a millisecond before he exploded down his sexy bartender's throat. He was sure a sound of some sort escaped his lips at the same time, but his orgasmic high was too intense for him to even give any sound he may have made a thought.

Chapter Nineteen

Travis' eyes never left his beautiful lover's face while he swallowed down Cal's pleasure. His own cock ached, throbbed painfully, but Travis didn't care. Seeing Cal fall into ecstasy and knowing he'd sent his bobtail there was the only thing which took up space in Travis' mind. Slowly, he crawled up Cal's body until his forearms rested next to Cal's pretty blonde-haired head. Travis patiently waited for his lover to open his eyes and finally focus on him.

"God," Cal whispered.

"No. I'm Travis," Travis replied just as softly with a grin and gave his lover a wink.

Cal snorted a laugh. He still felt like a limp noodle, but not so much he wasn't aware of Travis' jean covered erection pressing into his groin. The realization made him frown.

"What is it, pretty?"

Cal didn't reply, but instead tugged on the waistband of Travis' jeans and raised a brow. Travis chuckled, but before Cal could do more than tug on his belt loops again, his lover was naked on top of him. Cal was quickly coming to love Travis' vampire speed.

Cal thrust up. "In me." He pulled Travis' hips down to make his point.

Travis didn't need any additional encouragement to fulfill his lover's request. He grasped the tube of lube he had grabbed when he shucked his jeans. Travis wasted no time coating his fingers. He had to force himself to go slow while loosening up his lover. Apparently, Cal had other ideas. Travis barely breached him with a finger when Cal pushed down into his palm. Travis stilled his hand, but Cal didn't still his hips. No, he rotated them.

"Another," Cal demanded. "I can't wait."

"I don't want to hurt you," Travis whispered against Cal's lips before he added another finger.

"You're not," Cal replied and thrust almost harshly down into Travis' palm. "More."

Travis added a third finger and only thrust his hand a few times before he replaced his fingers with his cock. He pressed forward slowly, but shouldn't have bothered to worry about hurting his pretty garoul. Cal thrust up so harshly onto his cock that Travis practically shouted from suddenly sinking so deep into his lover's tight hot heat. Cal didn't give him time to recover from the shock which was purely pleasure induced before he moved again.

He had intended to make slow love to Cal, again, but Travis wasn't the one setting the pace of their lovemaking. Cal was and he obviously had no intention of taking things slow. In fact, it didn't matter Travis was topping his pretty man. No, because if either of them were fucking the other, it was Cal fucking him. However, this was more than just fucking. Cal was making love to him. Aggressively, but still making love to him. All Travis could do was kiss the man he loved and enjoy the ride of pure love and passion which Cal was taking him on. So, he did just that.

Travis' back arched and he exploded into his lovers welcoming heat way too soon. His head dropped to the crook of Cal's neck and it wasn't until he started to come down from his orgasmic high that he became aware of two things: slickness coated their abs which could only be the result of his lover getting off again and Cal's head tilted to the side in an obvious way to invite feeding.

Travis' gums itched and made his fangs feel like they were actually twitching. Still, he didn't assume his lover was offering to feed him again.

"Cal?" Travis whispered his beautiful garoul's name and his breath caressed his lover's neck while his lips caressed Cal's jugular.

"Please." Cal arched his head back further to the side. "Let me give you what you need."

Travis didn't *need* to feed again so soon after feeding from Cal the day before. Of course, that didn't mean he didn't want to feed from his lover again. Still, he paused.

"Travis."

Cal whispering his name with such need made him raise his head and meet his beautiful garoul's eyes. Cal had moved his head, so his gaze was leveled on him through a half-lidded gaze.

"Feed," Cal ordered before he closed his eyes.

Travis nodded his acceptance of Cal's offer even though his gorgeous bobtail wouldn't see the slight movement before he lowered his head back down, licked along Cal's throbbing jugular, and sank his fangs deeply into his beautiful garoul's neck.

Travis watched Cal sleep contently for a few hours. He could stare at his stunning bobtail for hours and not become bored with the view before him. In fact, several times he had told himself he needed to get out of bed and had every intention to do so, but hadn't been able to look away.

He did need to leave his lover in bed, though, so he gently forced himself to do so. Once he had extracted himself from Cal's embrace, his motivation to ensure his lover's safety from Hunters reasserted itself. Travis allowed himself one last long look at Cal before he closed his bedroom door and walked into his living room. He picked up his cell phone and hit speed dial.

Mikael answered before the first ring had even finished and Travis wasn't surprised his friend and boss picked up so soon.

"Brian checked our security feeds and didn't get much from them. I am calling in a specialist," Mikael said by way of greeting. "I will also be sending out Joshua, but I want a specialist here as well. I won't have one of mine threatened, especially outside of our club." Mikael's tone turned harsh, but Travis understood his friend's anger wasn't directed toward him.

"Who are you bringing in to track them?" Travis had asked for no other reason than Mikael used the word 'specialist' in reference to finding the Hunters who were threatening his lover."

"You don't need to worry about that right now," Mikael answered. "You just take care of your man and I'll take care of everything else."

Travis had no doubt Mikael would ensure his lover would be safe. Mikael made sure they were all safe.

"Okay," Travis agreed.

"I'll see you tonight," Mikael replied by way of goodbye and ended the call.

"It's my fault the Hunters are your problem now," Cal said with surety and didn't wait for Travis to fully turn toward him before he continued. "I need to just go."

It broke Cal's heart to say those words, but he wouldn't put the only man he ever loved and everyone who was so kind to him at The Witch's Brew in danger.

"They will follow me and you all will be safe."

Travis was in front of Cal and had him wrapped in his arms before his lover had even finished speaking. There was no way in hell he was going to let Cal run away again. Run away from the Hunters and him as a result when he could protect his beautiful bobtail.

"Do you trust me?" Travis forced himself not to squeeze Cal into his chest too tightly. He had to force himself to keep breathing while he waited for Cal's answer, as well.

"Of course, I trust you," Cal replied and had to force himself to continue to look into Travis' concerned gaze when he spoke again. "I think I love you, so of course I trust you. But that's why I should go. If anything ever happened to you," Cal couldn't stop the sob that managed to work its way around the lump in his throat from escaping his lips.

Travis pulled Cal closer to his chest and cupped his head against his shoulder. He tried to ignore Cal's suddenly rapid breaths which Cal ghosted against his bare flesh because every one his lover took broke his heart even more.

"If you trust me, let me keep you safe," Travis whispered against the top of Cal's head.

Travis did keep him safe. Cal had never felt safer in his life than when he was with Travis. Even being near the life drinker made him feel safe. Not only his human side, but his feline one, as well. Still, who would keep Travis safe if his father set his mind on killing him.

"I can't risk him hurting you," Cal admitted his greatest fear.

"Hey." Travis nudged Cal to force his lover to meet his gaze. "I've dealt with Hunters who are way more skilled than your father. Mikal has dealt with them in general for longer than I've been alive." Travis offered Cal a reassuring smile. "So, I'll ask you again. Do you trust me, beautiful?"

"I trust you, Travis, and I love you," Cal admitted.

"Then let me keep you safe because you're the first person I've ever fallen in love with and I won't let anything happen to you. I promise."

"You promise," Cal stated, not asked.

"I do." Travis cupped the back of Cal's head again to pull him close and encourage him to rest against his shoulder.

Cal believed every word Travis had just uttered with every fiber of his being. He still feared for Travis' safety though, but knew if anyone could provide safety for himself or Cal, Travis could.

"I love you, beautiful," Travis' voice was soft, but Cal had no difficulty hearing his lover's declaration.

"I love you, too," Cal replied and was more than sure their love would conquer any threat his father or Hunters might pose.

Travis would keep him safe.

Travis loved him.

Right now, that was all Cal needed.

Two days later…

The club wasn't very busy. In fact, Travis had no difficulty seeing the front door or the other two bars in the club through the patrons. That was just fine with him since it allowed him to see any trouble or danger before it reached his lover.

Still, that didn't stop him from looking over his shoulder at Cal. Travis had rearranged the liquor bottles on the shelf closest to the stool which Cal usually occupied. The shelf was just wide enough and high enough to give Cal space to lie in his bobtail form. Currently, that was exactly what Cal was doing. His lover appeared to be sleeping, but Travis knew better.

Travis had just looked away from his beautiful bobtail and across the bar when he spotted the last person he ever expected to see when Mikael mentioned bringing in a specialist. Shade.

He was aware his friend and boss took their family's safety seriously, but he never expected Mikael to bring in this kind of specialist. Still, seeing Shade casually leaning against Barb's bar in the corner allowed Travis to breathe easier than he had in the last three days.

Travis had no doubt his lover's safety would be ensured when Mikael sent Shade on the Hunters' trail. Still, that didn't mean Travis wouldn't remain hypervigilant to keep his lover safe and he had every intention of doing just that.

With a wide smile spreading his lips, he closed the few steps between himself and the dozing cat. His beautiful bobtail cracked an eye open when Cal sensed his approach. Travis didn't hesitate to run his palm down Cal's back from nape to nub.

"You're going to be safe now." Travis bent and kissed the top of Cal's fur covered head.

Cal pushed his head up into Travis' lips and purred deeply. He knew Travis would understand he was conveying his love the only way he could in his feline form.

"I love you, too," Travis replied and Cal's purr deepened and grew louder.

Travis didn't need to profess his love again because Cal had no doubt the life drinker loved him. And like two days before, that was all that mattered to Cal and all that he knew he would ever need.

ABOUT THE AUTHOR

Brenda is an Amazon international best-selling author for multiple titles and her love for reading fantasy, paranormal, and contemporary erotic romance has allowed the voices she hears to come out and play (according to her shrink, this is healthy!).

Brenda resides in Tampa, FL with her husband, six cats, a dog, a turtle named Tammy, and a bunny named Alice (only the cats are hers) when not attending conventions or leather/kink events. She is active in the Tampa Bay GLBT & leather community. Brenda is Ms. Florida Leather n' Fetish Pride 2016, the founder and organizer of Tampa Bay's Leather Social, and the owner and producer (since Jan. 2016) of the Florida Leather & Fetish Pride weekend event that is held every November in Clearwater, Florida.

She would love to hear from you! Visit her on the following:

Website: www.bcothernbooks.com
Facebook: Brenda Cothern Books
Facebook Fan Page: Brenda Cothern Books, Inc.
Goodreads: Brenda Cothern
Smashwords: BCothernBooks
Google+: Brenda Cothern Books
Twitter: BCothernBooks
Leatherpedia – Brenda Cothern
Authorgraph: BCothernBooks

For signed digital autograph, please send her a request through Authorgraph! Also, check out Audible.com for selected titles. If you enjoy her books, please show your support by giving it stars and/or writing a review on the various online retail websites.

245

GLBT Support Organizations

Brenda would like to acknowledge and thank MLR Press (www.mlrbooks.com) for compiling the below information on the various support groups.

THE TREVOR PROJECT

The Trevor Project operates the only nationwide, around-the-clock crisis and suicide prevention helpline for lesbian, gay, bisexual, transgender and questioning youth. Every day, The Trevor Project saves lives though it's free and confidential helpline, its website and its educational services. If you or a friend is feeling lost or alone, call The Trevor Helpline. If you or a friend are feeling lost, alone, confused or in crisis, please call The Trevor Helpline.

You'll be able to speak confidentially with a trained counselor 24/7.

The Trevor Helpline: 866-488-7386

On the Web : http://www.thetrevorproject.org/

THE GAY MEN'S DOMESTIC VIOLENCE PROJECT

Founded in 1994, The Gay Men's Domestic Violence Project is a grassroots, non-profit organization founded by a gay male survivor of domestic violence and developed through the strength, contributions and participation of the community. The Gay Men's Domestic Violence Project supports victims and survivors through education, advocacy and direct services. Understanding that the serious public health issue of domestic violence is not gender specific, we serve men in relationships with men, regardless of how they identify, and stand ready to assist them in navigating through abusive relationships.

GMDVP Helpline: 800.832.1901

On the Web: http://gmdvp.org/

THE GAY & LESBIAN ALLIANCE AGAINST DEFAMATION/GLAAD EN ESPAÑOL

The Gay & Lesbian Alliance Against Defamation (GLAAD) is dedicated to promoting and ensuring fair, accurate and inclusive representation of people and events in the media as a means of eliminating homophobia and discrimination based on gender identity and sexual orientation.

On the Web: http://www.glaad.org/

GLAAD en español:

http://www.glaad.org/espanol/bienvenido.php

SERVICEMEMBERS LEGAL DEFENSE NETWORK

Service members Legal Defense Network is a nonpartisan, nonprofit, legal services, watchdog and policy organization dedicated to ending discrimination against and harassment of military personnel affected by "Don't Ask, Don't Tell" (DADT).The SLDN provides free, confidential legal services to all those impacted by DADT and related discrimination. Since 1993, it's in house legal team has responded to more than 9,000 requests for assistance. In Congress, it leads the fight to repeal DADT and replace it with a law that ensures equal treatment for every service member, regardless of sexual orientation. In the courts, it works to challenge the constitutionality of DADT.

SLDN Call: (202) 328-3244
PO Box 65301 or (202) 328-FAIR
Washington DC 20035-5301
e-mail: sldn@sldn.org
On the Web: http://sldn.org/

THE GLBT NATIONAL HELP CENTER

The GLBT National Help Center is a nonprofit, tax exempt organization that is dedicated to meeting the needs of the gay, lesbian, bisexual and transgender community and those questioning their sexual orientation and gender identity. It is an outgrowth of the Gay & Lesbian National Hotline, which began in 1996 and now is a primary program of The GLBT National Help Center. It offers several different programs including two national hotlines that help members of the GLBT community talk about the important issues that they are facing in their lives. It helps end the isolation that many people feel, by providing a safe environment on the phone or via the internet to discuss issues that people can't talk about anywhere else. The GLBT National Help Center also helps other organizations build the infrastructure they need to provide strong support to our community at the local level.

National Hotline: 1-888-THE-GLNH

(1-888- 843-4564)
National Youth Talkline
1-800-246-PRIDE (1-800-246-7743)
 On the Web: http://www.glnh.org/
 e-mail: info@glbtnationalhelpcenter.org

www.ingramcontent.com/pod-product-compliance
Lightning Source LLC
Chambersburg PA
CBHW072216170626
46813CB00003B/967